BIRCH HILLS @ WORLD'S END

BIRCH HILLS AT WORLD'S END

ISBN:978-0-9819198-6-7

 **Vagabondage Press**
PO Box 3563
Apollo Beach, Florida 33572
http://www.vagabondagepress.com

First edition printed in the United States of America and the UK, September 2011

Also available in digital formats wherever e-books are sold.

10 9 8 7 6 5 4 3 2

Cover photo by Matt Brown. Front cover design by Maggie Ward.

BIRCH HILLS @ WORLD'S END

Geoff Hyatt

Vagabondage Press

.

1

irch Hills sprawled somewhere between Detroit and nowhere, and halfway through our senior year it started to break us. It was the ass-end of 1998. All across the country, lunatics stockpiled ammo and bottled water in preparation for a millennial apocalypse. The war with Iraq was brief and happened when we were little; you could still see shredded, yellow ribbons tied around backcountry trees. Our high school's doors stood unlocked all day; inside, it had no security cameras, and no one had to wear an ID badge. I had a mad crush on Lindsay Kruthers. Erik Grunder was my best friend. I'd never known anyone who got murdered. All of these things would change faster than I could have imagined.

The stereo system of Erik's Acura cranked out old Slayer songs at a volume that would have killed smaller mammals as we drove past the fast food pits and strip malls. Some of them had been decked out with Christmas lights, and their asphalt lots stood stark and black beside the snow. Erik smoked a joint, shouting to me between hits as he drove. I only caught every third or fourth word over the music: "...suspended...concert...bullshit... geometry...you know?"

I smiled and nodded. Sometimes he just liked to talk. Erik was smart, funny, and on the same advanced placement course track as me. He was also a hateful stoner who'd allegedly broke into the athletic office and crapped into the school mascot costume's head a few months before, an atrocity that went unnoticed until it was donned by Ashliegh Baer, the quarterback's girlfriend. This made Erik a hero to some, but an enemy to most, a position he accepted with pride.

After school that Friday, we headed out to the terrible waffle place at the edge of town to nurse cups of coffee for hours and maybe play cards. On my way out of school, I'd overheard Lindsay Kruthers telling her best friend that they were going to hang out there, too. I'd been trying to run into her after school for weeks, and it finally seemed like things were lining up. She was a bone-thin junior, known for cutting herself and writing bad rhyming poetry about killing her mom. She was also, by most accounts, the nastiest slut at Birch Hills High. She'd allegedly been kicked out of St. Margaret's for going down on a girl beneath the bleachers at a girls' lacrosse game. I was desperately in love with her.

I thrummed my fingers on the dashboard, the pounding music and bleak scenery adding to my unease. Lately, CNN had been buzzing about the Y2K bug, saying that all the outdated computer systems would crash in about a year, unable to deal with the zeros in "2000." Cars would pile up beneath malfunctioning stoplights. Power-grids would shut down, plunging cities into darkness. Planes would fall from the sky. These newly emerging zeros could cause every technological and societal disaster imaginable. I didn't want to believe I would survive four years of Birch Hills High only to see the world undone by bad programming, but I had to accept the possibility.

As the Waffle Palace came into view, I spotted someone in a pancake mascot costume by the roadside, a big, brown disc with fried-egg eyes and a bacon smile. Two round nostrils in the center of the pancake's face served as eyeholes. Erik waved and beeped his horn as we pulled into the Waffle Palace's lot. Pancake Man waved back.

The Waffle Palace had been a Chinese restaurant at one point, and the old sign still hung above the new one on the post outside. A tarp had covered it up for a while, but that blew away during a tornado warning last summer. Now, at a glance, the sign read: "Imperial Dragon Waffle Palace." When we walked inside, the waitress seated us and poured two cups of coffee.

"Hey, Doris," Erik said. "You look really good today."

She rolled her eyes and strode off without saying a word.

A string arrangement of "Santa Claus is Coming to Town" crackled throughout the empty restaurant. Inside, it seemed like Erik and I were the only two teenagers left on Earth.

I slouched in the booth and gazed out through the grimy window, waiting for Lindsay and her friend. My reflection superimposed over the parking lot: a lanky ghost with Kermit green hair and horn-rimmed glasses. Pancake Man danced and cavorted on the roadside while I sipped my lukewarm coffee. Mascots always bothered me, but I couldn't help staring at them. There was a real person inside that costume, probably sweating and angry and suffering. I always tried to imagine the human trapped inside a giant Chuck E. Cheese, Goofy, or in this case, Pancake Man. I would have rather died than put one of those things on. I was afraid, somehow, that I'd never be able to get out of it. That was my definition of Hell.

Erik busied himself, scrawling in his big, leather-bound journal with the restaurant's complimentary crayons. He claimed this "Doomsday Book" held his ultimate plan to destroy Birch Hills. I didn't know if he was kidding or not. As he scribbled away, his skin white as a bathroom sink, his hair sticking up all over in a black mess, and his T-shirt reading *Kill 'Em All*, he looked crazy enough to believe it. Bruises still blossomed around his jaw and left eye, stamped there by bunch of jocks in the Taco Bell parking lot. Erik had the nerve to flip them off after they called him a faggot.

"Shouldn't he be a waffle?" I asked.

Erik looked up, his crayon frozen mid-scrawl, his eyes bloodshot. "What?"

"The Pancake Man." I pointed to the window, across the parking lot, at the mascot. "This is *Waffle* Palace. Shouldn't he be a waffle, not a pancake?"

"Shouldn't we *all* be waffles?" he replied and then returned to coloring. I shrugged and slurped my coffee.

Car after car zipped past, taking no notice of Pancake Man. I finished the last of my coffee. There was no sign of Lindsay. After a while, a bus slowed down. It was a big blue-and-silver thing that reminded me of a Three Musketeers bar. The bus braked hard and made a wide, lumbering turn toward the Waffle Palace. I could tell the bus's front end wasn't going to clear a rusty hatchback in the parking lot. I lurched in my seat when driver's side corner of the bus smashed into the rear fender with a horrible, squealing crunch. Bits of the car went clattering and flying everywhere.

Pancake Man spun around to face the lot at the sound of impact. He took off at a dead run across the pavement toward the accident. Though his egg-yolk eyes remained wide and merry, and the bacon smile stayed frozen on his face, he was clearly pissed off. He dashed up to the bus and began furiously pounding and kicking its door. Waving one big, white-mittened fist at the driver, he thrust his other hand to point, as best he could, at the crushed car.

"Whoa," Erik said, gaping at the scene. "Pancake Man's gonna kick that guy's ass."

The waitress glanced up at the windows from behind her serving station but seemed as disinterested as ever.

"Bet it was his car," I said. "Probably be hard to fight dressed up like breakfast, though."

"I dunno. I bet he was pretty angry before, having to dance around and shit in the middle of winter. Now look at him. He's in a berserker rage."

"He's still smiling," I said.

"Yeah." Erik grinned. "This is gonna be sick, dude."

The bus chugged to a halt, belching a cloud of diesel smoke before coming to rest across the lot. Its tinted windows revealed only the shadowy forms of the driver and his passengers. Pancake Man awkwardly crossed his arms and stood at his full height. The bus's door folded open, and the driver cautiously stepped out

He was dressed from head to toe in shiny, plasticized armor the color of a hard-boiled egg. A sort of combination gas mask and helmet, all one piece, concealed his head and face. The guttering winter light reflected as irregular discs on his costume.

"Woah," Erik gasped. "The driver's a stormtrooper."

Yes, it was true. The driver was dressed as one of Darth Vader's innumerable and highly incompetent minions from *Star Wars*.

He held up his hands, as if at gunpoint, while Pancake Man hopped around and gestured wildly.

"What the hell is going on?" Erik asked.

"There's a science fiction convention in Royal Oak this week," I explained. "I bet they chartered a bus to go."

"You think the whole bus is full of them? Stormtroopers, I mean?"

"Maybe." I shrugged. "They form brigades for re-enactments and stuff. Like those Civil War weirdoes."

"Why would you want to do that? I mean, Confederates suck ass, sure, but at least they won some battles," Erik said. "Stormtroopers are losers who can't do anything right."

"Including drive a bus, apparently," I said.

Pancake Man shoved the stormtrooper, who took a step back, shaking his helmeted head.

Erik banged rapidly on the window, bouncing in his seat and yelling, "Pancake Man! Strike him down! Let the hate flow through you!"

The waitress ignored us, but Erik's noisy bloodlust drew the Waffle Palace manager, dressed in a stained white T-shirt and apron, out of the kitchen. He was an old, chain-smoking Greek with a gray push-broom mustache. A fading cobalt tattoo of a dagger through a heart covered one of his massive forearms. The manager never spoke English and rarely had a facial expression. He strolled to the window beside our booth, placed his hands on his hips, and watched. Pancake Man shoved the stormtrooper again, with both hands this time, nearly knocking him over. He regained his balance and shoved Pancake Man. The manager raised a bushy eyebrow. Erik giggled.

Pancake Man hauled off and threw a white-mittened fist as a solid jab into the stormtrooper's throat, just below the facemask, sending him reeling into the side of the bus before dropping to the icy pavement.

"Damn!" Erik and I cried.

A massive cadre of stormtroopers poured out of the bus like a white amorphous blob and swarmed Pancake Man. The manager took three great strides across the dining room and then hollered something in Greek through the kitchen door. A mob of tattooed swarthy dudes followed him out into the lot to defend their mascot. The skinny guy at the rear carried a mop slung over his shoulder. It was like the dugouts emptying at a baseball game. A giant pile of stormtroopers, Greeks, and a lone anthropomorphic pancake were beating the holy snot out of each other between the tour bus and the ruined hatchback.

"Screw this," the waitress said. "I'm going home." She vanished through the kitchen door.

With the rest of the staff brawling outside, we were left there all alone.

"This," Erik said, "might be the coolest thing we'll see in our lives."

"It's definitely up there."

A stormtrooper kicked Pancake Man in the nuts and then was brained with a mop handle. Erik stared out the window. He turned back to me, his face baleful and serious.

"But what does it all mean?" he asked.

"What does what mean?"

"This." He pointed out the window.

I nodded. It was a matter of existential importance.

"It means," I said, "that when conflicting fantasies collide, the result is mutual destruction."

"No." Erik waved my idea away. "No, that's not it."

A stormtrooper's helmet sailed through the air and thunked against the window.

"It means," he said, "that in a world populated with Pancake Men, stormtroopers, and Greeks, mankind will never know peace."

A police car rolled into the lot. A cop jumped out, ran up to the fray, gaped at it, and then ran back to his car. A few seconds later he returned, holding a baton in one hand and a video camera in the other, smiling.

"It means," I said, "we can get free refills of our coffee. There's no one left to watch us."

"Yes. I think you've got it. They should be happy we're not

cleaning out the register."

A police van pulled into the lot, lights flashing, as the combatants continued pummeling away. Erik brought the coffee pot from behind the counter and refilled our cups.

"While good men die," he said, "rats get fat."

We sat there in the Waffle Palace as the first canisters of teargas detonated outside. A light snow began to fall, the flakes shimmering in the blue police lights. Billowing fog obscured the unlikely war just beyond our window, and we sipped on the dark bounty of their conflict.

"Finish up," Erik said. "I gotta meet Kenzie at the park downtown."

"Hey," I said as I pulled on my coat, "you have any idea what Lindsay Kruthers is up to tonight?"

2

A lot of kids used to hang out in the back lot of the Gas-Go until it was outfitted with loudspeakers that blasted classical music. Erik forecasted that this modification would lead to a cultural renaissance: a generation of kids who would associate Mozart with weed and hand jobs. A similar technique had been used downtown a year before, where recorded hawk calls were used to frighten off sparrows. Both the symphonic music and the raptor cries eventually proved too much for their targeted species to endure.

Erik and I weren't officially affiliated with any group. Smoker's Corner, across from Wolf's Lair Tattoos, remained the domain of the auto-shop burnouts and glue-huffing punks who lived in the trailer park by the highway. Future teen pregnancies and house arrests, all. Erik bought weed from them sometimes, but they weren't really our speed. Preps and jocks, who hated us, held the multiplex, which the wiggers drove circles around in their neon-accented Escorts and Civics, booming rap music; the geeks gathered in the nearby strip mall at the comic shop, where they played collectible card games and argued about science fiction; the skaters loitered in the small, two-level parking structure beside the hospital, where cops periodically showed up to hassle them for trespassing. The Gas-Go was a free zone for everybody.

Erik and I were there one hot night last summer when I first fell for Lindsay Kruthers. We were stoned and sitting on his back bumper. Six different car stereos battled in the packed lot, rapping and howling, booming and thudding. Clouds of bugs swarmed the greenish lights above. Lindsay came out of the Dairy Queen across the street, barefoot, carrying a pair of knee-high boots in one hand and a strawberry sundae in the other. When she and her friend Amanda ran out into the street, a car jammed on its brakes and blared its horn. They shrieked with laughter, and a bunch of the kids in the lot cheered. Lindsay curtseyed and gave a black-lipsticked smile. She had a plastic spoon tucked behind her ear. After that, I just couldn't stop thinking about her.

Now, a few months later, the snowy lot was abandoned on a Friday night, and Lindsay was nowhere to be found. Erik parked his Acura at the public library, and then we trudged through a playground toward our spot, the snow crunching beneath our shoes. Christmas carols, weirdly disembodied, echoed through the winter air. Erik raised his whole arm to jab his finger at a small, light-bedecked structure. It stood before the planter we usually sat on—and it hadn't been there yesterday.

"Oh, no," I said. "Not here."

We took off at a dead run toward it, like soldiers storming the beach, until at last, we stood before the new Yuletide horror of Birch Hills.

A red and green plywood gazebo stood before us, sheltering a band of life-sized Victorian carolers. Concealed gears and wiring gave them a crude semblance of life. Their arms rose and fell. Their heads looked left and right. Their mouths opened and closed, poorly synchronized with holiday music that blasted from a spookily unseen source. The fabric of their period clothing juxtaposed against their plastic skin only emphasized the eerie fakeness of it all. Now that the park held a bunch of happy, singing androids, yet another of our habitats had been destroyed.

"Jesus. This town exists only to torment us." My words came out as clouds of vapor, fogging my glasses. "Can you believe this?"

Erik sat down on the concrete planter. With a flourish, he lit a smoke before holstering the Zippo back inside his motorcycle jacket.

"You know how this will end, Josh," Erik said, jerking his head toward the carolers. "Soon, these robots will rise up and kill their masters. Ever see *Westworld*?"

"*Westworld*? No. I've seen *Blade Runner*, though. It always goes down the same." I sighed. "It's cold. Let's go."

"We gotta wait for Kenzie. He's supposed to have something for me."

"Why do we need to meet him here? It's not like this is some out-of-the-way location. We're downtown. This is stupid."

"Kenzie is stupid," he said. He took a long drag from his cigarette and then flicked it at the caroler-bot with the walrus mustache, striking its stovepipe hat. The carolers responded in unison by poorly lip-syncing "Joy to the World." We both burst into laughter.

Erik said, "We need a new place to loiter."

"What in the hairy shit are those things?" bellowed a voice behind us. We turned to see Kenzie weaving his way across the park, his dress khakis soaked to the knee from snow, the front of an untucked Oxford shirt hanging out the bottom of his ski-jacket like a loincloth. Tommy Li, a friend of ours from school, followed him like a footman.

"Those," Erik said, nodding at the carolers, "are a twisted mockery of Christ's birth. It's their only redeeming quality."

"Fucked up," Li said. His voice was deep and melodic, like a cello. I couldn't tell if he was referring to the display itself, Erik's evaluation of it, or his own sobriety. Li was always cool. He never smiled.

Kenzie half-stumbled over to me and punched my arm. His laughter reeked of whiskey, and his stubble was flecked with gray.

"Ow! Dick!" I snapped. "Don't you have any kids your own age to play with?"

"*Don't you have any kids your own age to play with?*" He mimicked me in a lisping girlish voice. When he smiled, he had a little boy's face with the crow's feet and laugh lines of an old man. At twenty-seven, he was the butt of plenty "old man" jokes. "Why are you such a faggot, Josh? You worried I'm gonna steal Li away from you?"

One night, a couple years before, I drank a few bottles of Boone's Farm wine and told everyone I'd totally want to sleep with Li if I were a girl. I don't know why I said it. He had nice skin, a rich gold color, and wore big diamonds in his earlobes. Li dressed a like a rap star, and we called him "Chigger" sometimes, after he pointed out an Asian couldn't really be a wigger. I was wasted when I said the thing about sleeping with him. And I had added the qualifier about being a girl. It was hypothetical. I was still living down the gay-bashing. Li was cool about it at the time, at least. He'd only said, "Thanks, I guess."

"What's with that one?" Kenzie pointed at a caroler, the little apple-selling urchin who gibbered along to "Frosty the Snowman."

"The guy with the top hat is his pimp," Erik said.

"He's also selling apples to help fund his deviant lifestyle," I added.

Kenzie pulled an engraved silver flask from his back pocket, spun off the cap, and took a long swig. "Why's he the only one with dirt on his face?"

"Well fucking duh, Kenz," Erik said. "He's supposed to be *poor*."

"What the hell do I know about being poor?" He took another swig.

Kenzie was technically named Charles Edmund McKenzie. The *Third*. Heir to the McKenzie Jewelry business. A college dropout and a total alcoholic druggie, yes, but never one hurting for money.

"So, you got it for me or what?" Erik asked.

"Nope. But you can get it tonight, if you want to meet me at a party."

"Where at?"

"My friend Jason De Groot's house."

I shuddered. I didn't know what the two of them were trying to exchange, and I didn't care. But Jason had been a linebacker for the varsity squad before I even moved to Birch Hills, and his brutality remained legendary, both on and off the field. A drunk driving accident had cut short his full-ride scholarship to U of M, as well as some poor guy's life.

"I thought he was in prison," Erik said.

"Parole," Li intoned.

"That's right, Chigger. Good behavior, no priors, all that."

Kenzie chuckled. "He and I roomed together at U of M. Jay's a good dude. A bit of time in the joint and getting his leg crushed in the accident really chilled him out."

"Somehow, I doubt that," I said.

"Shut up, Joshie. Why is your hair still green?" He batted at my head, but I ducked. "Green hair, horn-rims, and a tweed coat. What are you supposed to be, anyway?"

"Gee, Kenzie. Does this mean we're not friends? I don't think I could bear that."

"Whatever." He capped his flask. "You losers want to go to this party or what?"

"I'll call you later," Erik said. "But you better have something for me if we go."

"Something?" Kenzie laughed. "Shit, there'll be more somethings than you can deal with out there. It's Jason's coming home party, bro."

3

I was not cool with going to a party honoring an ex-jock ex-convict known for beating up people and vehicular manslaughter. But the fact was I didn't have a car, and neither did much of anyone else I hung out with. If I didn't go out to the party, Erik would drop me off at the comic shop or somewhere until my mom could pick me up. I was a senior, so I'd rather die than let that happen on a Friday night. But more than that, there would be no chance of running into Lindsay Kruthers if I took the geek route. I told my mom I was going to the movies with Erik, and then I'd be hanging out at his place. A few hours later, I was a county away, out in the freezing dark of Butt-Fucking Egypt. Party time.

Erik's black Acura sat parked on the shoulder of the road, as out-of-place as an alien starship. I gaped at the scene through the car's smoky window. The house looked like a post-apocalyptic Alaskan farmstead: a rickety two-floor Victorian, blanketed with snow. Strips of paint hung from its siding like a birch's peeling bark. Shadow-people drifted through the yellow eyes of its windows. In between this slanting monstrosity and a pole barn were parked several cars, pickups, and motorcycles. Some had tire tracks trailing behind them from when they'd been driven and parked in the yard. Others had no wheels or windows, and lurked as rusty bodies caped in white. A tattered Confederate flag hung from the porch railing.

"You have got to be kidding me," I said.

"Oh, don't be so bourgeois."

"Excuse me?"

"It means—"

"I know what it means," I snapped. "I just think it's funny you're seventeen and driving an NSX, calling *me* bourgeois."

"Exactly. If I can deal with it, why do you have to be so…classist?"

"You're right," I said. "Many people with Confederate flags on their porches and broken-down cars in their yards have done a lot for this country. Maybe there'll be a cross burning later."

"Actually," Erik said as he unfastened his seatbelt, "it's called a cross *lighting*."

"It's sad that you even know that."

"Goddammit, Josh." Erik clambered out of the car. "Are you coming or what?"

"Fine."

"This is a bad idea," I said as we walked onto the stoop. I heard the overlapping shouting of party people, like animals in a barnyard, through the door. "What if the beef-patrol that jumped you at Taco Bell is here?"

"Doesn't look like their scene, really. We're not even in the same area code anymore. If they're here, though, I'll probably stab them."

"Great. I refuse to hide out in some abandoned church and read *Gone with the Wind* to you, afterwards."

"I'd hope not," he said.

Erik knocked on the door, and a few seconds later, it swung open, revealing the giant figure of Jason De Groot. The guy filled the doorway. He was as barrel-chested and towering as I remembered him, but that's where the similarity ended. His blonde hair, once in a buzz-cut, now hung in dirty dreadlocks past his shoulders. Even though it was mid-December, he wore baggy cut-off cargo shorts and rubber flip-flops. I could see the brace around his right knee, all plastic, metal, and Velcro. Bloodshot eyes peered at us through the folds of heavy lids, a pink film over blue. Jason leaned heavily on a cane whose cap was a grinning golden skull.

A deep baritone rumbled from the corner of his mouth, "Whattup? You Kenzie's friends?"

"Yeah," Erik and I said simultaneously.

We said stuff at the same time a lot, which I always found embarrassing.

"Well, shit!"

Jason stepped to the side and swept his arm with a grand gesture into the overcrowded room beyond. With the cane gripped in his other fist, he looked like an albino Rastafarian ringmaster, luring us into his demonic circus.

"Welcome to the Farm, bitches!"

Erik strode past him and into the place like a returning war hero. I shuffled after him. It smelled like damp cigarettes and diesel fumes and was so packed that I could barely breathe. Through gaps in the crowd, I glimpsed tattered beer posters and magazine centerfolds tacked to the walls. Some hardcore music pounded as an overdriven mess from the stereo. Jason seemed friendly enough. He hobbled behind us, pointing at various people and telling us their names, but I couldn't hear most of it over the loud music and jabbering voices. There were plenty of faces I recognized.

Until now, I had always wondered where all of the wrecked rejects went when life drove them from Birch Hills. People like Sam Colly, a kid with acne scars like napalm burns, who went to juvie after trying to torch the concession stand. Or Chris Spitz, Alan Spitz's older brother, who came back from Desert Storm with stories of burying people alive, along with some mysterious illness he couldn't beat. Girls like Rachael Golding, who took some E at a house party, and then had the video of her ensuing threesome with a couple of nasty nu-metal douchebags seen by thousands on the Internet. They were the kind of people nobody knew, but everyone knew about. Birch Hills was a conservative, well-to-do place where, according to the sign downtown, "Quality is a Way of Life!" I had assumed damage-cases like these people always ended up moving to New York or California.

Now I knew what actually happened. They ended up out here. And now I was with them, too.

I shouldered my way through the crowd. Erik had brought me here; I couldn't lose track of him at the party. Without me, he'd have no voice of reason. Without him, I'd have no one to drive me.

If we got separated, neither of us might ever make it back home.

The hordes thinned out a bit in the kitchen. Li sat at a scratched-up table playing spades with two girls I knew from school. One was Amanda Gates, who cursed like a trucker and whose thong underwear always stuck out from the back of her low-cut jeans. The other was her best friend, the terrifyingly beautiful and endlessly mysterious Lindsay Kruthers.

Lindsay stared down at her cards. I had never seen eyes so green or so distant. Her pointy nose, atomic red hair, and matchstick body fused fragility with danger. I stood awestruck, captivated by the little whips of hair on the back of her neck.

Erik leaned over the game, watching as if he had money placed on the outcome. He punched me in the arm and nodded toward Lindsay. My stomach twisted.

"Um," I said. "Hey, Li. Hi, Linds."

Li nodded. Lindsay's eyes flitted up at me, and she gave me a little half-wave before looking back at her cards.

"Aren't you going to say 'hi' to me?" Amanda asked, pouting, her long, horse face looking up at me from her chair. She got on my nerves. Everyone called her Annoying Amanda for a reason.

"Hi."

She smiled. "Your hair looks really good blue."

"Thanks," I said. "It's green, actually."

"I'm color blind," she tittered. "But I have a really good visual sense."

I shifted from one foot to another, not sure what to say or who to talk to. I realized I was staring at Lindsay, but she was staring at her cards, so she didn't notice.

"Jesus, play a card, you stoned twat," Amanda shrieked and then burst into a fit of laugher.

Lindsay played a card. Erik stood across the kitchen, talking with Jason and some mulleted guy who looked like Frankenstein's monster. A bald eagle with an M-16 in either claw emblazoned the front of Frankenmullet's T-shirt. Jason looked amused, and the monster looked brain-dead. I caught Erik saying, "A fuckin' stormtrooper, for real." Jason laughed. The monster did not. I stayed where I was.

"So, hey, Lindsay," I said.

She looked up at me, and I became locked in her emerald gaze. My limbs froze up, my words evaporated, and my dick stirred. One corner of her thin mouth pulled into a smile. "Yeah?"

Nothing came to me but panic. Fortunately, the monster in the eagle T-shirt bellowed "Freedom!" at the top of his lungs, like William Wallace, and then smashed an empty beer can against his head. That pretty much got me off the hook.

Jason and the monster plowed past the table and headed out the back door. Erik was right behind them. He grabbed me by the shoulder and pulled me along, out the door and onto the porch. Li and the girls followed.

Some skaters from my silk screening class were out there already, sitting in a semi-circle and passing around a bong. One of them, Devon, looked at me from the tattered recliner he was sitting in and blearily said, "Hey." Jason poked him in the belly with his cane.

"Get the fuck out of my chair," he said to Devon.

The skater kid made a show of leaping up and sitting on the porch. His friends laughed. Jason eased himself into his now-vacant throne. He gestured for the bong with one hand while flipping open the beer cooler beside him with the other. Li stood with his arms folded across his neon-yellow Fubu jersey. Lindsay and Amanda sat down Indian-style in the circle, then made room so Erik and I could join in. Frankenmullet lumbered away, stepped off of the back porch, and then vanished around the side of the house. He even *walked* like he was sewn together from ten different dead people.

"This is good shit," Jason said as he handed me the bong, which had been rather expertly fashioned from a Chia Pet. "René's shit."

I didn't usually get stoned. I wasn't too eager to be the four-hundredth person to place my lips on the drilled-out asshole of a clay sheep, either, but I was afraid to say no to Jason. Even crippled, he looked like a real bad guy to piss off. I accepted the bong and pantomimed flicking a Bic with my free hand. Erik tossed me a lighter, which I managed to catch, for once.

I hit the thing and, when my thumb came off the toke hole, instantly felt like I'd been kicked in the chest. I doubled over in a fit of coughing. Acrid smoke spewed from my mouth, nostrils, and I think even my ears. I tipped the bong and the Chia Pet vomited swampy water into my lap. Erik smacked me on the back a few times. When my fit subsided, the circle was still laughing about it.

"That'll open up some lung sacks," Jason said.

He lifted the bong to his lips and took his hit from the snout end. I felt deeply ashamed of having opted for the sheep's ass.

I burped. A wispy gray cloud of pot-smoke escaped.

"Aw," Lindsay said. "That was cute. Like Baby Godzilla."

I felt my cheeks burn and looked at my Vans.

So then everybody talked about the standard shit they do when they party on a back porch in the country: movies, gossip, music, drugs, et cetera. I tried to look like I was following. Now and then, my wandering gaze caught Lindsay's eyes, and she'd smile. My head was in a bucket, and the words I wanted to say seemed to gather in my stomach rather than come out my mouth. The cold concrete slab of the back porch numbed my ass. I gathered my flimsy tweed coat around me and shifted with discomfort.

The brown ends of cornstalks jutting from the snow-blanketed field behind the house made it look like a giant's stubbly cheek. A scrawny dog wandered across that bleak face, silhouetted in the moonlight. I studied this scene, trying to divine its significance, rapt in what it all meant to my shivering self at that moment.

"Fuckin' dog!" Jason yelled as he yanked a beer from the cooler's ice. "Watch this."

He chambered back his arm, then threw the unopened beer can as a perfect spiral pass. It arced high into the winter sky, like a mortar shell, and then hurdled down, cracking the shadowy mutt in the head. A distant metal clank accompanied a sharp yelp. The dog took two steps to the left, one to the right, and then fell over, now only a dark heap on the snow-covered field. I was completely horrified.

The rest of circle laughed uproariously, except for Li and Lindsay. It made me feel really sick. I mean literally. I thought I was going to puke, and my chest felt all tight like it does before my asthma kicks in. I stood up and wandered off the porch, mumbling something about going to take a piss.

I found a spot between two tall bushes beside the house and edged into it. I leaned against the house and took a deep breath. The moon was so bright and big that night; it was crazy. I had a clear view of the yard and pole barn in front of me, but my hidey-spot was inky dark. I imagined I was a ninja. That calmed me down a bit.

Erik was probably trying to work Lindsay while I was gone. Asshole. He got with plenty of girls, and most of them were cute enough. I didn't understand why a bad-tempered destructive smartass hooked-up all the time. It made no sense at all. Maybe it was the car.

A rampaging Chevy pickup interrupted my brooding before I got too depressed. It tore across the yard with its headlights off, bouncing over the hills and spewing snow out the wheel wells as it skidded to a stop. The giant chrome bumper halted a little under a half-foot from the pole barn's door. Kenzie, laughing maniacally, jumped out of the cab. I crouched down in the bushes, hoping I wouldn't have to talk to him. I didn't recognize the guy who half-fell out of the passenger side. The truck was about thirty feet away, but I could tell this dude was really pissed off.

"I'm not getting deported for your stupid bullshit, Kenzie!" He slammed the door. "You are understanding this, motherfucker?"

He had an accent; his soft *I*'s came out as long *E*'s, his *th*'s as *Z*'s. *Bull-sheet. Muzza-fuck-aire.* Probably French. I thought it was hilarious, and the fact that he was angry made it even funnier to me. I bit my lower lip to keep back the giggles.

This guy was at most five-foot-seven, and his shoulders seemed as wide as he was tall. His legs, wearing drainpipe jeans tucked into engineer boots, looked absurdly skinny when compared to his overdeveloped torso and arms. His head was shaved, and he had a tiny, black mustache. Seriously. As he stalked over to

Kenzie, I noticed the crossed six-guns airbrushed on the back of his leather jacket.

He snatched Kenzie by the shoulders and shook him. "Kenzie, the line, it has been crossed! You go far from me now!"

Kenzie's lanky beer-bellied frame thrashed around like a ragdoll in a dryer, but he kept laughing. "Don't you feel *alive*, dude?" he asked. "Admit it, René, you got to!"

So *that* was René, the man's whose product filled Jason's lung-crushing Chia bong. He let Kenzie go then twisted one end of his mustache between his thumb and forefinger, nodding.

"All right, yes. It was fun. But people will notice he is gone, no? Tomorrow morning. They will come looking for him, and then, they look for *us*."

Nobody from the party came around to see what was going on. The noisy misuse of Kenzie's life had ceased to be a spectacle for most people a long time ago. Besides that, I had a feeling that most of this crowd had seen things a lot more screwed up than another rich kid gone rotten.

"René, if the shit goes down, I'll take all the blame. I swear."

"Okay, bro, okay. It is cool," René said, "but we hurry to get him out of the back of your truck, no?"

Kenzie awkwardly climbed into the back of his pickup, tripped over something lying in the truck bed, and then stumbled over to the tailgate. He opened it while belting out N.W.A. lyrics in a disconcertingly accurate imitation of Ice Cube.

"Enough of that," René snapped. "You get the head. I'll get the feet."

Kenzie shoved something over the tailgate. René took one end and Kenzie the other. Wrapped in a plastic shroud and bound with rope, it looked like a body.

Oh, my God, I thought. *This is* not *happening*.

4

I'd never thought Kenzie was a psychopath. An accident waiting to happen, sure, but not a time bomb. Now, watching him and a French drug dealer drag a tarp-wrapped body out of a pickup, I wondered how I could have been so wrong.

"This little man," René said with a laugh, "he is somewhat heavy."

"Dead weight," Kenzie grunted as he struggled to keep his end of the load up. "We need to go to the door around the other side, before the little high schoolers see this. They'll freak—*whoa!*" Kenzie burst into jackal-like laughter and said, "His arm, dude!"

I could see it, hanging out from under the tarp, its stiff fingers dragging in the snow. I swallowed the scream quaking in my throat. I had no idea what these guys would do if they discovered me but was positive I didn't want to find out.

"This is—errrmmmmm—morbid," René grumbled. "I am not needing this."

Snowflakes flitted in the moonlit air, like glitter on glass. Kenzie and René, rendered in a palate of grey and blue, lugged their dark cargo around the corner of the pole barn. The door creaked open then slammed shut, loud as a shotgun in the winter stillness. The December wind sliced through me.

I'd fled a dead dog only to encounter a dead man. I only came to this awful party because of Lindsay, who Erik was probably fingering in a coat closet by now. A sour taste washed into my mouth. Hyperventilating and dizzy, I staggered out of the bushes.

"Josh, don't worry. He's not dead," said a girl-voice behind me.

"What?" I shouted as I spun around.

Lindsay stood there in her cloak, smoking a black cigarette from a long, brass holder. She looked like a thrift-store version of a thirties crime dame, afflicted with vampirism. A big army-surplus ammunition bag hung on her hip, on which she'd stenciled the words "KILL YOURSELF, NOW." I appreciated her use of a comma. She wore one of those furry hats, the kind that usually make people look like puppy dogs, but it worked on her. The smoke she exhaled smelled like my mom's Easter ham.

"The dog that Jason hit with the beer can," she said. "He got up and ran off. I think he was just knocked out for a bit. No big deal."

"It's still mean," I said, shuffling in place. I made a tiny white wall between my feet.

Lindsay laughed, lovely and quiet. "*Everybody's* mean," she said. "C'mon. I got to get inside or Amanda's going to get drunk and take off her shirt or something."

"Yeah." I took another deep breath. "Yeah, okay."

As we began to walk, I considered telling her about the crime I'd just witnessed but thought it might be a bad idea. After all, maybe it was just a passed-out friend they were playing a prank on. Maybe.

"Your cigarette smells like ham," I said and then considered punching myself in the face for being such a dumbass.

"They're cloves," she said. "You must be freezing."

She said the last part like a movie line and looped her arm around mine. Instant hard-on. I stuck my free hand in my pocket and managed to push it into the twelve o'clock position, the best method of concealment.

Even though Lindsay was finally paying attention to me, I couldn't stop thinking about that stiff arm dragging through the snow and Kenzie laughing about it. I had to tell somebody, but I didn't want to ruin my chances with Lindsay, and I was scared. I realized this probably made me a bad person, but I couldn't help it. We went back into the house together.

The rest of the party was a weird mix of high school shenanigans and white trash mayhem. For the first time, I realized that the main difference between these two things was the age of the person doing them. If you see a fourteen-year-old light his fart and laugh, it seems normal. Seeing a thirty-five-year-old do it seems messed up. Same thing with getting into fistfights, bonging beers, passing out and making out in public. All of the kids and adults were doing the same things, and it seemed disturbing in every case, because no one seemed to know what was okay and what wasn't, or what to do about it, or maybe just plain didn't think there was any difference.

Jason patrolled the party, smoking a blunt and jabbing at some of the more unruly guests with his cane. After downing their forties of Mickey's, the skater kids did a pretty hilarious improv of a pro wrestling smackdown, which ended with Devon getting a folding chair cracked over his head. Some old guy with a white beard and a fringed Daniel Boone jacket cleaned out the cut with 151 proof liquor and stanched the bleeding with what looked like a pretty professional dressing. Annoying Amanda made out with a guy decked out in whiteboy cornrows, black raccoon make-up, and wide-legged, plastic pants with neon blue flames printed on them. Then she threw up and lay on the floor, moaning about how she wasn't supposed to drink on her medication.

Soon after, Erik punched that same goth-raver-cornrow guy in the mouth for making fun of Iron Maiden. This earned him accolades from a pack of grizzled bikers, who all wore jackets with the word "Leatherwolfs" and Nazi SS runes across the back. They had stomped into the scene around one a.m., greeted by Jason and Frankenmullet guy with much noisy hollering and bro-hugging. Cornrow guy took off. Erik smoked a joint with the bikers. I wondered why anyone would choose to be a biker in Michigan, where the climate meant you could only "live to ride" a few months a year. Of course, I was as likely to ask them that as I was to correct their pluralization of the word "wolf."

Not long after the bikers showed up, some wasted girl with short, black hair and a lip ring made out with Erik in what I was sure would be a tonight-only feature. Tommy Li rode away in his souped-up Honda Civic with some blonde hottie in ass-tight stonewashed jeans, which was a pretty odd paring. I couldn't help notice, much to my relief, that none of the white-power bikers gave Chigger a second look. Throughout all of this, Lindsay clung to me, giggling and whispering in my ear about the way whiskey made her face feel hot, like she was leaning over a bonfire, or how the curve of her waist fit perfectly against my hip. I hadn't had much to drink, but I was intoxicated.

Eventually, Kenzie came in to the kitchen, walked over to Jason, and put his arm around him.

"Where the hell you been, bud?" Jason asked, smacking him on the back.

"Jay-boy," Kenzie said. "You got to padlock that barn door."

Jason looked down to check his fly.

"No, dude, not your pants," Kenzie said. "The barn, bro, the barn."

"Why?"

"C'mon, I'll show you."

They walked out the back door. The fingers of the body under the tarp, dragging through the snow, flashed in my mind. I started shaking.

"Are you okay?" Lindsay asked me.

"I don't feel good," I said. "I really want to hang out with you, but I don't feel good right now."

"Well, go home, then," she replied. "The party's breaking up, and I probably should get Amanda out of here, anyway. We can hang out sometime this week, I mean, if you want to."

"Really?"

"Really."

Erik stood with his back turned to us in front of the kitchen sink. I called over to him.

"Erik, do you want to, um, roll out pretty soon?"

He turned around, a goofy sneer frozen on his face, and glassily stared at Lindsay and me. He was pale as a ghost, save the myriad bruises on his face.

"I'm still pretty wasted, but okay." Then, he walked over and whispered in my ear, "I'll meet you in the car. Let you have a second alone, eh?" He nodded at me and ambled off.

I turned to Lindsay, who looked up at me with those gorgeous emerald eyes and gave me a tiny smile. My mouth was dry and my tongue felt three sizes too big.

"So," I said. "I, uh, I had fun hanging out with you tonight."

"Me too."

"And you still, you know, want to do something later this week?"

"Yeah. Yeah, I'd like that."

"Well, I still have your number from that time I asked you for it." I stuffed my hands in my pockets.

"You mean last summer? Really? You never called."

"Yeah, uh," I said. "I was pretty busy. My family went camping, and I, well, you still want to do something this week? Like a movie or something, maybe Tuesday? Because cross-country season is over, so in the afternoons, or the evenings, you know we could—"

Lindsay grabbed me by the back of the head, pressed her face against mine, and shoved her open mouth over my lips. Her tongue tasted like liquor and cigarettes as it made frantic circles in my mouth, like a wet, ashy pinwheel. It was the most unbelievably hot thing that I could've possibly imagined. I grasped her bony shoulder blades and pressed her against me. I didn't want it to ever end, but I was getting low on air. Every time I tried to breathe though my nose, it made this funny whistling sound, so I gently stepped away.

Crimson lipstick had smeared all around her mouth and jaw. She looked like a white wolf cub glancing up from her kill.

"Call me," she said.

"Okay," I replied.

We hugged once more before I walked out to the car.

On the drive home, Erik had the stereo turned down to a comfortable level so he could concentrate on the road. Neither of us said anything for a while. I tapped my fingers nervously on the center console.

"Will you stop *tapping*? You've been doing it all day." Erik growled. "It's really annoying." Then he added, "I'm not mad at you, you know."

"For tapping? It's not like I was doing it on purpose."

"No, not for the tapping, you retard," Erik said as he navigated the curves of Edgemoor Drive. "For getting with Lindsay. I'm not mad."

"Why the hell would you be mad?"

"I'm *not* mad. That's the *point*," Erik said. "Look, I only said it because you're all quiet and seem upset."

I suppose I should have said, "Erik, I finally hooked up with Lindsay, but the fact that she hangs out at places like 'the Farm' makes me feel even more uncomfortable about liking her than I did in the first place. I'm upset because I spent the evening at an ex-con's party, full of old burnouts exploiting minors for fun and profit. But what's bothering me more than anything is that I saw Kenzie and a French drug dealer hide a dead body in a barn. My sense of moral responsibility is at odds with my desire for gratification and my instinct for self-preservation, and it's all a bit much for me to deal with right now."

Instead I said, "I'm tired."

"I'm wasted," he replied.

"You're driving."

"Yeah. Well." He shrugged. "There are worse things I could be doing. It's not the end of the world."

We rode in silence for a bit, the deep drone of Erik's music mixing with the whir of wheels on the road. The fields and woods outside were dark as a cave, the night forming a tunnel around the car as it sped through the countryside.

"Do you think the world is going to end?" I asked.

"Eventually," Erik replied, as if this were a totally normal thing to ask out of nowhere.

"No," I said. "I mean soon. Like when the millennium comes."

"Sure. And the dead will rise for Final Judgment, and unclean spirits will leap like frogs from the Mouth of the Beast."

I shuddered, imagining the little man in Jason's barn, wrapped up in a tarp and rising up before the Lord. I imagined God to look like a toga-wearing Santa Claus.

"You don't really think that."

He laughed. "Of course not. The universe doesn't know what time it is or what fucking year it is. That's people shit. Not, like, cosmic shit, you know? Since when did the universe care what people think?"

"Yeah."

Birch Hills came into view. It sprawled across the valley, originally a farming town built around a grain mill on the Mokqueta River years ago. Not that you could tell that now. The lampposts of the multiplex theater, strip malls, and major streets diffused an orange stain of light across the sky. From the country highway, on the outskirts, thousands of little Christmas bulbs burned as multi-colored threads; they shone, tangled in distant tree branches and wrapped around snow-topped houses. Common as it was, Birch Hills seemed an oasis of light against all of the cold and night we'd driven through since going to the Farm. I thought of the newscasters' talk about the Y2K bug, of car accidents, system crashes, and power failures. I worried.

I got home a little after two in the morning, past my curfew. My family lived in a decent two-floor, four-bedroom house in the Whispering Meadows subdivision. Mom drove a Honda, Dad a Toyota, two sensible cars that slumbered in a cute, little garage. We didn't have any Christmas lights outdoors. Dad called them wasteful; Mom called them tacky. Our Christmas tree, however, blazed in the front window. That meant Dad hadn't gone to bed yet. He always unplugged it before he turned in.

My parents never locked the front door. I crept inside, keeping the knob turned and gently shutting the door behind me. In a single motion, I slipped out of my sneakers and shrugged off my coat and scarf. I turned to hang up my stuff on the coat tree, and nearly jumped out of my skin.

Silent as winter, my dad stood in the middle of the family room. His hair was messed up, and he didn't have his glasses on. He was nearly taller than the Christmas tree, looming, with his head titled all the way back, staring at the ceiling. The tree's bulbs threw the only light, like a giant candelabrum, pitting his eyes with shadow.

"Dad?"

He didn't look away from the ceiling, but he raised a hand with his fingers splayed and said, "Quiet."

Dad got weird sometimes, especially at night. He was an insomniac. Back when we lived out in the country, he used to walk the edges of our property in the middle of the night or stare out the windows like a dog waiting for the mailman. Now he mostly hung out in his basement den after Mom went to bed, building model airplanes, listening to scratchy blues records, and drinking Millers. Staring up at the ceiling in our front room was a habit I hadn't seen before.

"Joshua," he whispered. "Come here. Quiet."

I obeyed, my stocking feet stepping around the sofa and standing beside my father. He hadn't looked away from ceiling, so I stared up at it, too. It was plaster and looked like swirled cake frosting.

"Listen," he said.

I didn't hear anything. I thought for a moment that maybe Dad was drunk, or maybe he'd finally gone off the deep end after years of bland eccentricity. And then I heard it.

A scratching, scrabbling sound, the noise a shadow would make if it wanted to scare someone, or the way grave dirt would whisper. My dad and I stood side-by-side, looking up at the sound.

"There," he said. "Do you hear it?"

I shivered. "Yes."

"Thought I might be going crazy," he said.

"No. I heard it."

"It's in here," he said. "Tunneling. It found a way inside."

My blood froze and my heart galloped. The man Kenzie had in the tarp was dead. I was kidding myself to think otherwise. Something horrible happened out at the Farm, and it followed me home, burrowing and creeping into the foundation of where I slept. I stood closer to my father, enough to feel his warmth, and knew I would tell him. I'd tell him about the truck and the barn and the hand dragging through the snow. My silence had brought a ghost into our home. He could help me put it to rest.

And then Dad said, as if he'd just solved a grand riddle, "It's Chippy."

Chippy was a fluffy, brown squirrel. Our front yard's hickory tree dropped hundreds of nuts in the fall, and Chippy had hung out in it for years. We all thought he was cute and would point and laugh as he bounded around the branches. Now, it seemed he had chewed his way into the attic and begun stashing the nuts inside our house's walls and ceiling.

"Oh."

My desire to confess now seemed shameful and foolish. I felt as far away from Dad as I had felt close just a few moments before. I tried to tell him anyway.

"Dad," I said, "tonight at the party—"

"Party?" He cocked his head and frowned. "I thought you were going to the pizza place and over to Erik's."

"I was, I mean I did, but—"

"Have you been drinking? Erik didn't drink and drive, I hope." He looked down his watch, grumbling. "You're late for curfew. Go to bed."

"But—"

"Joshua. Go to sleep." His voice hardened. "It looks like we have something to take care of tomorrow."

5

I woke up at about eight the next morning. Silvery light streamed in through the blinds. Lying on my side, clutching a pillow to my chest, my mind struggled to separate dream from memory. Lindsay's kiss. The body in the snow. Erik and me in a sleek, black car, talking about the end of the world. I sat up and rubbed the sleep from my eyes.

The world hadn't visibly changed. A plastic Godzilla still stood on top of my dresser. The same thumbtacks (yellow, plastic) held up the same posters (The Clash, Subhumans, Wolverine, Kurt Cobain, *Blade Runner*) on the same painted walls (reddish brown). My hockey stick leaned in the corner, sheathed in dust. A cheap bass guitar sat propped up against an even cheaper amplifier. A wooden plaque with a Tolkien quote ("Not all who wander are lost…") burned into it, made by my older brother in eighth grade wood shop, hung beside the door. It didn't seem like any of the previous night's events happened at all, or maybe they transpired in a world that evaporated in daylight.

Then I heard the noise. The sound of that animal rummaging and rustling in the walls could not have been any creepier. Chippy had kept me from sleep for most of the night. I knew it was just a squirrel, but the thought of something hidden, just beyond the surface of my walls, freaked me out—especially since its source seemed so harmless at first.

The scratching noise died down when I kicked off the covers and got out of bed. Waking up early on weekends frustrated me. Every weekday, I was booted out of torpor by an alarm clock, followed by my mom yelling up the stairs for my whimpering sister and me. Then I was forced to eat oatmeal or waffles or whatever when I wasn't even hungry and shipped off to school. Every weekday morning, I would have given about anything to have just a few more minutes of sleep. When the weekend finally rolled around, with no alarm clock, whining sister, or yelling mom, I woke up at the butt-crack of dawn anyway. I never could get back to sleep.

I pulled on a pair of pants and a sweatshirt, and then plodded downstairs, resigned to look at birds with my parents and watch cartoons with my little sister. Maybe I'd play some video games.

Mom sat on the couch by the Christmas tree, holding a cup of coffee and gazing out at the birdfeeder. Her glossy hair caught the front window's light, seeming platinum rather than steel gray, gathered in a loose bun. She had her little half-glasses on, too, completing what Dad called her "school marm" look. She usually didn't let down her hair or put in her contacts on weekends, and I think it bugged him a bit.

"Morning, sunshine."

With a grunt, I sat down in the puffy chair across from her. I pulled a copy of *Time* from the perfect fan pattern of magazines on the coffee table between us. A little kid's face with the word "RITALIN" beneath it filled the cover. I yawned and put it back.

"The new *Time* is in the bathroom," she offered. "Your father's at the store. I made waffles for Alison already. I put the extras in the oven."

"I'm not hungry," I said.

"Well, they're in the oven. Probably still warm."

"Thanks."

"If you plan on getting one, you should have it when they're still warm. They don't reheat well."

"Jesus Christ," I sighed.

She blinked, startled by my annoyance, and then looked glumly into her coffee cup. I felt bad. We had this conversation, or some version of it, countless times. As usual, I went into the kitchen and got the waffle I didn't want. Alison was playing with her dolls during a commercial break in the living room, making them talk to one another about going to the beach. I liked hearing her play.

"The good syrup is still out on the table," Mom called from the front room. "Butter, too."

I returned with my plate and a glass of juice to the front room and sat down to look out the window.

"We get another cardinal?"

"Yes. A male. Look at him, red as a berry. And not as many of those nasty blue jays this year to chase the others away."

"Is that fat one a dove?"

"Sure is. Wonder where his wife is. They mate for life, you know."

"Maybe he doesn't have one."

The birds flitted and fluttered around the feeder beneath the hickory tree. Seed shells, like black pebbles against the snow, formed a ring around its post.

"Erik and I saw a guy in a pancake costume get into a fight with some dudes dressed up as stormtroopers yesterday."

I explained what happened to her as best I could. At the end of it, she asked me, "Shouldn't he have been a waffle?"

"That's what I said."

"Hmm." She sipped her coffee. "What did you and Erik end up doing last night?"

Before I could answer, a shape the color of dried blood swooped down toward the birdfeeder, like a kite caught in a downdraft. When the hawk made contact with the doe-eyed dove, its talons tore into smaller bird's plump body. With a few beats of its muscular wings, it carried off its prey. All of the other birds fled so quickly, it seemed they'd blinked out of existence.

A cream-colored feather spiraled once in the air before coming to rest on the snow.

"Awww. Poor guy." My mom clucked her tongue then looked over to me. "That's the third time this week."

"What?" I said. "Since when did we have hawks?"

"We've always had hawks, Josh." She sipped her coffee. "You just see them more now. They used to nest up on the hills by the lake and in fields out on Edgemoor Drive. I suppose all that new construction has pushed them out here."

"Oh."

"It's probably why Chippy burrowed into the attic."

"Because of the outlet mall they're building?"

"Because of the hawks."

I stood up and took my waffle plate with me, feeling a bit nauseated. Mom must have noticed, because she called after me, not unkindly, "Joshua, it's just a part of nature, that's all."

It wasn't the hawk that bothered me, or how the dove bought it right there while I ate my breakfast. It was what I'd seen out at the Farm the night before. I needed to tell someone. On the other hand, I knew what happened to snitches in crime movies and didn't want to end up run through a wood chipper or sunk to the bottom of a river. Also, if a story like that made it back to my parents, there was no way they'd allow me to hang out with Erik, Lindsay, or much of anyone else for a long time. I figured Erik would be a good, or at least trustworthy, advisor on this. Unfortunately, he wouldn't be waking up for a few more hours.

I never worried about murder in Birch Hills. I mean, there were plenty of fights between kids, lots of broken wrists and bloody noses, but no real gang shit. A group of wiggers at school called themselves "The Ca$h Flo Kings." They drove their tricked-out rice burners around the mall parking lot, occasionally graffiti-tagging the dumpsters behind the multiplex as if this were somehow desirable and disputed territory. One town over, a group called "The Green Lake Pimps" ruled over a carpool lot with similar tactics. The two factions raced each other on backcountry roads once in awhile, which I thought was lame as hell.

There were plenty of guns around, but nobody ever got shot. Most adults in Birch Hills were white, Republican football fans who considered themselves tight with Jesus, which meant nearly everybody's dad had at least two guns. Even Erik's dad, an aging hippie songwriter who wore a beard and little, wire-rim glasses and who gave money to Greenpeace and Earth First and all that, had two old Soviet assault rifles and a Mauser in his attic. Erik showed them to me once, saying his dad kept them around in case of "total societal breakdown."

The only gun we had we had was a CO2-powered Daisy BB rifle my older brother, Paul, got for his tenth birthday from Uncle Pete. He was only a year older than me, but this made him the test case for every rite of passage.

I think Uncle Pete had hoped to initiate Paul into the family tradition of deer hunting, a big deal on Mom's side. He would have had an easier time convincing him to cover his face with Maori tattoos. At ten years old, my brother carried spiders outside the house rather than kill them. He was so socially awkward that people thought he was autistic. He had asthma even worse than I did, he looked at his feet when he talked, and he aspired to both be a computer programmer and become fluent in Elvish. He'd never be in a deer-blind before dawn, tell dirty jokes around a campfire, or sleep on the ground. After seeing the genetic precedent set by my older brother, Uncle Pete never even bothered with me. The air rifle gathered dust in Paul's closet.

He'd left home to study engineering at Michigan Tech last year and was due home from school in about a week for Christmas vacation. I was looking forward to it, but also in a way I wasn't. I had thought he was the coolest guy in the world at one point, and still sort of did, but it didn't feel like we'd grown up together anymore. Or rather, like he hadn't grown up at the rate I had. We still had a blast talking about all the comic-book sci-fi fantasy stuff we always did, but I'd acquired some interests now that Paul had little to say about. Like politics, music, and girls. Still, I missed him.

The dark-blood shape of the hawk surfaced in my mind again as I rinsed off my breakfast plate, which brought back the trophic pyramid from middle school science class. *Everything eats everything else*, I thought.

I wanted to watch some Saturday morning superhero cartoons, but my little sister remained absorbed in one of those horrible big-eyed Japanese cartoons starring schoolgirls and fuzzy animals. I ended up doing a crossword at the kitchen table, pleased to know a five-letter word for the Norse gods. Eventually, Dad came home with a Bigmart bag, which he plopped down onto the kitchen table, across from me.

I looked up and reached over to the bag, pulling down one corner. It held a box of BBs and a CO2 canister.

"Are you going to—" I started to ask, remembering Paul's air rifle.

Dad shushed me. He jerked his head toward the family room, where Alison lay on her stomach in a pink jumper, watching cartoons. Mom now sat in the rocking recliner beside her, absorbed in an Amy Tan novel.

I nodded. "Can I come?"

I don't know why I asked. I didn't really want to. I guess I just thought I should be with him and not downstairs with my mom and sister.

"I don't see why not," Dad replied. "He's in the tree right now."

I picked up the bag, and then the two of us crept upstairs to Paul's room. It looked pretty close to the way it did before he went to college. Pictures of nebulas and spaceships covered the walls. The room used to be that gross, dark orange color people liked in the seventies, but Dad repainted it before we moved in. The color Paul picked, according to the little paint chip sample, was called "Deep Space Blue."

Dad opened the closet. He bent over to remove some dusty boxes of comics and a bucket of plastic dinosaurs. Then he stepped inside the closet, hunched over in that tiny dark space, and emerged with the gun.

He knelt down, resting the rifle's butt on the floor with its barrel pointed toward the ceiling. With a nod, he pointed to the bag dangling from my right hand. I passed it over to him.

I looked around Paul's deep blue room. The mattress was bare. Tiny Japanese robots stood on a shelf over the headboard, brandishing little swords and guns in frozen poses. A poster on the wall behind them showed the whorl of the Milky Way, a creamy cyclone on a sea of black. An arrow pointed to one of the galaxy's innumerable white specks. Printed beside it were the words "YOU ARE HERE."

Dad's hand rustled in the plastic bag. The BBs clattered into the air rifle, and then the CO2 canister snapped into place. I turned to see him leaning the gun against the wall beside the window. He looked over at me and held his finger over his lips: *shhhh*. Then he pointed to the hickory tree beyond the glass.

He gripped either side of the window frame and slid it open without a sound. Naked branches scraped against each other outside. An icy breeze crossed my face, sharp with frost. My spine prickled when he reached for the gun. I crept closer.

Chippy the Squirrel scampered in the tree's upper boughs, nearly level with the window. The branch dipped and swayed under the rodent's thick, brown body like a telephone wire in the wind. His tail was a bushy question mark. Little feet scuttled against the bark, the same claws I'd heard behind the walls last night.

Dad stood like a statue, the gun propped against his hip. His face was stone.

In a single motion, he stepped back, placed the rifle stock against his shoulder, and jabbed the barrel out the window. He sighted his target with his eyes open, his body rigid and frozen, like a life-sized version of a plastic soldier. It looked wrong because it looked so easy, so automatic, as if he'd rehearsed killing that squirrel hundreds of times before that moment.

The gun coughed, a sharp burst of air, the sound of someone spitting dirt from his mouth.

Chippy dropped and tumbled end-over-end. I couldn't see him land from where I stood. Dad lowered the rifle but then abruptly lifted it again to peer down its sights.

"You got him," I said. "Wow, Dad. You're a good shot."

The gun dropped to his side when I spoke, as though it weighed a hundred pounds. He looked at me through those thick glasses as if he didn't recognize me for a second. His lips pressed together into a wide, upside-down V. His Adam's apple bobbed down, then up, above the neckline of his sweater. He tilted his head to one side and blinked.

"Yeah, I know," he said at last. Then he added, a bit tersely, "I joined the army in '68, son."

"You said all you did was type and file."

"I still went through Basic," he said. "Everyone did."

"Oh."

He sat the gun down and said, "Would you mind taking care of the body out there?"

"No problem." I did mind, actually, but I didn't want to disappoint my dad.

When I picked up the dead rodent, it was somehow both stiff and rubbery, its tail straight and springy like a car antenna. Even though my hand was wrapped with newspaper, it made me a little sick. I tossed Chippy's earthly vessel, along with its *Detroit Free Press* shroud, into the curb cart.

I needed to do something about what I'd seen at the Farm. In a clear blue sky, the sun was white and cold. I began the walk over to Erik's house.

6

*e*rik Grundler and his family lived in the exclusive Shady Glen community connected to my subdivision by a short, tree-lined boulevard but separated by an automated road gate, as well as a few income brackets. Fortunately I was on foot, so I could just duck under the gate without needing an access card. Some security.

As I entered Shady Glen, my cell phone rang. It was Lindsay's number. I took a breath and tried to collect myself, hoping to sound nonchalant. I even let it ring a couple more times before answering. We chatted as I plodded by the giant McMansions, watched by the unblinking eyes of artificial reindeer, snowmen, and several nativity scenes from various yards.

It was an awkward conversation. Lindsay and I talked about how we both had fun at the party last night, even though there were some creepy people there. At last she told me of the night's great tragedy.

"I left my hat there," she said.

"Your Russian hat?"

"Yeah," she said. "Look, I really hate asking this, because I know it's out in BFE, but I wondered if you could give me a ride out there later."

"Well…"

First of all, I never wanted to go out to the Farm again after what I'd seen. Secondly, of course, I didn't have a car. I did have a license, but my parents never allowed me to use either car for more than an hour. Before I could even think about what I was saying, I told her, "You can ride out there with Erik and me later."

"You guys are going out there?"

"Yeah," I said. "We were going to, you know, hang out there later, anyway."

I couldn't stop the train now and hoped I could deal with the wreckage afterward.

"Really?" she asked. "When are you heading out?"

"Oh, I don't know. I'm on my way over to Erik's right now. I'll give you a call to get directions before we come over to pick you up."

"Sweet." Her voice smiled. "I know we just saw each other last night, but it'll be cool to hang out again, don't you think?"

"Yeah. For sure."

When she said goodbye, I clicked off the phone, slid it into my pocket, and then slapped my hand against my forehead.

Erik's house loomed on the hill above. It looked more like a ski lodge. The winter sun reflected off the roof's black solar panels. It was an eco-friendly "green home," custom built to his parents' specifications. Erik once called it "the Taj Mahal of hippie guilt."

I suppose it wasn't an entirely unfair assessment. Erik's dad was Don Grundler, a musician whose band had a Top 40 hit with the catchy folk-pop ditty "(Come on) Join the Daisy Chain" in the late sixties. The money from this allowed him to buy a friend's failed artist commune about ten years later. He rented it out as a summer camp for a while and later sold a big chunk of it to developers. The developers turned it into the Shady Glen gated community.

Shortly after that, a major label hip-hop artist lifted and looped the guitar hook, along with Don singing the words "Come on," from "(Come on) Join the Daisy Chain" without permission. The rapper's label handed over a huge settlement. Erik sometimes joked that his dad had made a deal with Satan, the conditions being that rather than serve time in Hell, he would have to enjoy his fortunes in Birch Hills.

I rang the doorbell, and Erik's mom let me in. She had long, black hair, riven with gray. I never made eye contact with her. Mrs. Grundler was always overly nice to me because she thought I was really shy, but really it was that I thought she was really hot and felt gross thinking that about my best friend's mom. She always asked about my asthma. Once when I was sick, she gave me a packet of some foul tasting herbal tea, which actually made me feel better. Mrs. Grundler complimented me on my green hair and told me Erik was downstairs in the rec room.

I found him standing over the ping-pong table, which he had converted into a miniature landscape. Over the past few years, Erik had covered it with tiny trees and grass, rocks and mountains, glaciers and dunes. Among these schizophrenic ecosystems stood a medieval castle, an Aztec ziggurat, a modern airstrip, a stretch of World War I style trenches, and a seashore with a Viking ship—almost all of which he'd carved from foam rubber, Styrofoam, and plastic, then hand-painted.

It was a playing field for a game called All Guns Blazing, or AGB, in which various miniature armies battled down to the last man. We used to play it together all the time but hadn't so much since our sophomore year.

"Seeing that fight at Waffle Palace yesterday made me think about setting up the game again," he explained.

"Whatever happened to the new battlefield you were going to make?"

"Oh, I'm still working on it." He smirked. "It'll be awesome. Wanna play a game now? You can either be Vikings and aliens or Saracens and robots. It's already set up."

"I don't know. Maybe later." I flopped down into a beanbag chair.

"Awww, Josh," he said with mock concern, "is something wrong? Are you too grown-up to play AGB? Do you have sand in your vagina?"

"Shut up. This is serious." I sighed. "I need your help with something."

He made an adjustment to the Viking ship as he asked, "What's up?"

"Lindsay called me while I was on the way over here."

"Wow. Less than twenty-four hours. She totally wants your cock."

"You shouldn't talk about her like that."

I knew if I started dating Lindsay, plenty of people would be sneering about it. She'd hooked up with a lot of people. Not any more than a slew of other girls at school, though. Unlike Ashleigh Baer, or Alyssa Whitman, or the rest of the student council and cheer squad mafia, no one thought people wanted Lindsay because she was desirable. It meant she was easy.

"I like her," I said. "A lot."

"I like her, too. Lindsay's cool, but I mean, she's, you know—" He must have seen how upset I was getting and paused. "I just don't want you getting all dramatic about it," he said.

"Yeah, well, she said she needed a ride out to the Farm later, and I told her that we were going out there already and would pick her up."

"I don't really know those guys much better than you do," Erik said. "I mean, why does she need to go out there?"

"She left her hat there."

"That Russian one?"

"Yeah."

He shrugged. "As long as we have an excuse to go, fine. But don't volunteer me to taxi your ass around anymore without asking."

"Well, that's not the only problem," I said. "I saw something bad go down out there last night. Something I wasn't meant to see. Like a, um, murder. I think."

"No shit?" He smiled, his teeth like military tombstones. "Tell me about it."

So I did. It all just poured out of me: the pickup, Kenzie, René, and the arm tumbling out from under the tarp. Everything. After I was done, I hunched forward, pressed my face into my hands, and rocked back and forth in the beanbag.

"What am I going to do?" I moaned. "What the hell am I supposed to do about this shit?"

"Wow." Erik scratched his head. "I wonder if that's why they didn't have the gun I wanted."

"What?"

"I was supposed to buy a nine off of someone out there, but Kenzie said they had to get rid of it. Maybe they used it to off somebody and had to ditch it."

"Huh? What did you want a gun for? The next throw-down at the Dairy Queen? Jesus."

"I have my reasons."

I rolled my eyes.

"Look, Josh," Erik said, "showing up there to get Lindsay's hat today is a great thing."

"What? Are you crazy?"

"Totally fucking crazy, but that's not the point," he said. "Listen. There's no way they'll suspect you saw anything if you come back the next day and act all normal, right?"

"I don't think they suspect anything now, anyway."

"You can never be too sure." He squinted, scrutinizing the little battlefield. "It's a good chance to be casual."

"What about the guy in the tarp?"

"What about him?"

"Well, if there's a dead guy out at the Farm," I said, not sure why I had to explain this, "shouldn't we call the cops?"

"Uh, no," Erik said. He moved a robot figure onto one of the castle towers and then looked up at me. "Point A: It won't change the fact that the guy's dead. Point B: It might change the fact that we're alive."

"I thought you weren't afraid of anything."

"If you wanted to testify against Kenzie, Jason, and that Frenchman, you know, whatever, fine. I'm not particularly attached to them. But you might be testifying against those Leatherwolf bikers, or Travis, or God knows who else." Erik grimaced.

"Who the hell is Travis?"

"The big dude with the eagle shirt and the mullet. He's kind of a somebody out there. Not a good dude to piss off. I really don't have time to make a new best friend before we graduate."

My stomach sank. "You wouldn't be my friend anymore?"

"No, I would." He shrugged. "But you won't be much fun to hang out with after they kill you."

My skin rippled with chill.

"Promise me you won't tell anyone," Erik said. "Please."

I pushed my fingertips under my glasses and pressed them against my eyelids.

"Fine," I whispered. "Fine."

We picked Lindsay up around seven. She lived in one of the small, cracker-box houses off of Main Street, a cheerful blue place with white trim. Honestly, I'd expected her to live in the trailer park since she hung out with Amanda Gates and felt bad about assuming that. She came running out and gave me a big hug then clambered into the cramped back seat area of the sports car. She had to sit sideways across both seats to fit. We listened to music too loudly to talk on the drive out there, but Lindsay played with my hair from the back seat (instant hard-on) and Erik passed a joint around, which I pretended to hit. I didn't need to seem any more awkward and paranoid than I already was. My life might depend on it.

The Farm, without all of the cars parked out front, looked even more desolate than it had the night before. The yard was all torn up from being parked on, crisscrossed with footprints and tire tracks, littered with bottles and cans. We parked out on the shoulder of the road.

We walked up and knocked on the door, and it swung open almost immediately. Jason glowered down at the three of us, his face nearly veiled by greasy tentacles of blond hair. He turned his back and hobbled away, leaving the door open behind him. We all exchanged looks before following him inside.

The room reeked of sour apples and tar, of stale vomit and burnt hair. The radio, tuned halfway between two stations, played a garbled and fuzzy mix of a guitar solo and some pop dance music. Jason loped away from us across the living room, moving in slow motion like that old Sasquatch footage they always show in documentaries. His skull-capped cane leaned in the corner, a gilded shrunken head on a stick.

The place had been messed up even more since last night. Some girl's pants were in a crumpled pile on the stairs. Fist-sized holes riddled the walls, like the room had been strafed by a tank's machine gun. Kenzie and René sat on the couch, both of them so soaked in sweat they looked like melting wax statues. Kenzie's hair gel had turned to glistening slime, and dark stains soaked the pits of his dress shirt.

Fat, oily beads trickled down René's forehead and face. He stroked his damp mustache with a leather-gloved left hand. A butane torch roared in his right. He waved the demonic blue flame against a glass tube on the end table. White lines of powder sat on a foil sheet before them. My heart quickened.

Erik, Lindsay, and I stood like nervous pigeons in the front room. A pistol-shaped ashtray overflowed with cigarette butts, and the air was thick with smoke. René picked up the tube with his gloved hand and then used it to suck up one of the lines, the hot glass turning the powder to smoke. Jason glassily stared across the room at us.

"Hey, guys, what's up?" My voice was grating and chipper.

Kenzie winced. René exhaled a cloud of smoke white as swan's wing. Roiling and lazy in the air, it was almost beautiful.

"I think the real question is what's up with you?" Jason said.

"Me?" I said.

"Lindsay left her hat here last night," Erik said hastily. "We just thought we'd roll by and pick it up."

"So you think you can just 'roll by' here, uninvited, whenever you want?"

"Ummm." Erik faltered for a second, "We could just go—"

"You know, there was a time when I'd beat the shit out of guys like you just because I could," Jason said, staring up at the ceiling. "Little fags like you thought they were so above it all, and I'd show how none of them were worth shit."

"Nope, no hat here, sorry to have bothered you," I said. "Let's go, guys."

"You are not needing to leave yet," René said. His lips were split and peeling, his voice black as a swamp.

"People used to love me for beating the shit out of freaks," Jason continued. "It made them feel better about being normal, regular people. You know? All I did was fuck up losers, nail hot bitches, and play ball. King of the world, bro, king of the world."

I trembled. Lindsay put her hand in mine and whispered, "He's all fucked up."

"Goddamn right I'm all fucked up, you cunt," he snapped. "Six surgeries on this leg, sixty-two staples and two metal rods, and three years in the fucking pen on top of it. I'm on enough fucking shit to kill everyone in this room." He leaned forward and glared at Lindsay. "*You got a problem with that?*"

René burst out into yipping laughter, like a hyena. The sound of it pulled my ball sack tight.

"Could you guys check the volume a bit?" Kenzie's face twisted with pain. "I'm heading to crash city. Head's killing me."

"Oh." Jason sat down on the floor, leaning his back against the wall with his crippled leg stretched out in front of him. "Sorry, bro. It's just…" He trailed off, looking around at the ravaged walls and ripped up carpet. "I never thought I'd end up out at the Farm. Shit."

"You wanna stay in the coach house at my folks' place?" Kenzie asked. Jason waved him off.

I moved to the door, my hand locked around Lindsay's. Erik stood looking with his head tilted to one side at Jason, as if he were trying to decipher a sign written in a foreign language.

Kenzie called out to me, "Hold up, Joshie. We know what you saw last night. If you try to leave, you'll never make it."

My blood froze. I wanted to run but felt like I was in one of those dreams where your legs won't move and your mouth can't scream. It didn't matter, because Travis the Frankenmullet stomped down the stairs and stood in front of the door, staring us down with dead, gray eyes.

"Josh," Lindsay whispered, her voice quaking, "you're going to break my hand."

I let it go, saying, "Look, guys, we're not here to get in your business."

"Too late," Travis drawled.

It was the first and the only time I'd hear him speak.

Jason awkwardly found his feet again and pointed his cane at us. "Everyone's involved now. So you might as well see him, just so you know."

René cackled. "To the barn!"

They herded the three of us outside, Travis watching from the porch with his arms folded, the king surveying an execution. I couldn't believe this was actually happening. Jason led the way. Kenzie and René flanked Erik, Lindsay and me. Each step brought us closer to the barn's door. Its tall, narrow planks, held together by two fitted, crossed boards, made it look like a coffin lid. We stood there, trembling, before the splintering planks and rusty hinges. Jason unlocked the thing, and we all trundled inside. The door slammed shut like a slaughterhouse gate behind us.

I blinked rapidly, my panicked eyes darting around until at last they adjusted to the light. Kenzie slumped in the seat of a riding mower in the barn's corner, a beer in his hand, laughing at us. Jason stood beside him, leaning on his cane, rubbing his eyes with one hand and shaking his shaggy dreadlocked head. René loomed behind us. Everything smelled like pot and sawdust.

We were going to die. They would kill Erik and me, then rape Lindsay. Rusty pitchforks, scythes, and vises filled the filthy shed. I remembered the butane torch inside. We were going to be tortured first, I realized. We'd become a *Time* magazine story about meth and rural savagery, our three faces above some header like *HORROR IN THE HEARTLAND*. I could imagine the whole thing, from beginning to end, and there was nothing we could do.

I don't think I was crying, but I kept repeating, "You don't have to do this," in a toneless mantra, until Jason yelled at me to shut up. I pushed up my glasses and shivered. Erik arranged his leather jacket and cleared his throat. Lindsay buried her hands in the pockets of her coat and looked at the floor.

"Well, guys, I hope you realize what you've gotten yourself into, poking around in our business," Jason grumbled. "Now you're involved. You ready?"

Before I could shout my refusal, Erik said, "You don't scare me, Jay. Do what you got to."

"Well, come on then."

René gave me a little shove from behind, so I followed as Jason ushered everyone to the far end of the barn. We approached a workbench covered with a black plastic tarp. A brown-shoed foot stuck out from one end. I shambled forward, zombified by fear.

Jason stood before the workbench's shroud like it was a sideshow attraction. He pointed his cane's golden skull at us and said, "What you are about to see may shock you. I know it surprised the shit out me."

Kenzie giggled.

"You can look, but you must swear never to tell anyone about this," he continued. "If you do, I'll have René chop you up and throw you in the swamp. Right, René?"

"I am a very sick man, yes," he replied, folding his arms.

"You have our word as outlaws," Erik said.

"Alright," Jason said. "Let's do this."

He gathered the end of the tarp above the body's head in his fist. It crinkled and shifted. He whipped the plastic shroud off the workbench with a single motion, like a stage magician, and shouted, "Ta-Daaaaa!"

I only caught a glimpse before I clamped my hands over my eyes, shouting, "I don't want to look! I don't want to look!"

Everybody laughed an avalanche of overlapping hysterics— even Lindsay. It was insane, how fast things could go from good to bad, and I just couldn't deal with it. She rested on hand on my shoulder and squeezed it. "Josh," she said. "It's okay."

I just kept saying, "I don't want to look," like a broken record, shrill and pleading.

"Listen," she said. "You can look. It's not what you think."

I heard Kenzie's stupid chuckling as I slowly lowered my hands from my face. Erik patted me on the back. I opened my eyes and looked at the workbench.

He laid there, with his blue eyes unblinking, his mouth hanging wide open, in his patched-up grey knickers and little brown shoes. His little English hat sat crookedly on his head, and his box of fake apples rested on his chest. Cables and wires trailed from his back and hung over the side of the workbench.

It was the little urchin from the Christmas display in the park.

Relief flooded through me, and my grin spread so wide that my face nearly split.

"I nearly shit my pants!" I yelled at Kenzie.

"I know, dude, I know," he said.

"This," Erik said, "is demented in a good way."

"He was very heavy," René said. "Kenzie, he try to take the one with the big hat, but could not carry him. So he roll him into the pond."

"You killed his pimp," Erik said. "Like *Taxi Driver*. Cool."

"I just thought Apple Boy, you know," Kenzie said, "I thought he deserved a better life. I thought he'd want to come party with us."

Jason grinned, quite pleased with the scene.

"Listen," he said, thrusting the cane at us, "Don't tell *anyone*. People are going to go apeshit over this."

"We won't," I said, still shaking my head in amazement.

"Alright," Jason said. "Now get the hell out of here, before your moms come looking for you."

As we headed out to the car, Jason bellowed after us, "Merry Fuckin' Christmas!"

I was embarrassed that Lindsay had seen me so afraid, but she still played with my hair from the back seat all the way home and said she'd see me Monday at school. On the ride back, I watched Erik by the stereo display's blue light, the dark hollows of his eyes fixed on the road. He wore a wistful smile as he sang along with the music of anger. The black metal vocal screeched, *This is the end of everything...*

The leather seat creaked beneath me as I sat up straight. I couldn't let myself get too comfortable. We didn't have far to go.

7

The abduction of Apple Boy was front-page news, at least as far as the *Birch Hills Observer* was concerned. Chubby cheeked, with his mouth open in mid-song to form a perfect O, he looked like a disturbing sex doll in the paper's lead photo. Above this, a headline shouted, *Where's Apple Boy?* The Birch Hills Chamber of Commerce offered a reward for any information leading to the animatronic caroler's recovery. Police derided the "Grinch" who, by stealing such a valuable ornament, had not only shown a lack of holiday goodwill but committed a felony as well.

Also featured on the front page were a zoning board meeting, a car accident, and something about how to make gingerbread houses.

"A felony?" Erik shook his head and laid the paper out on the lunchroom table. "Can you picture going away for that? Criminal Kidnapping of a Christmas Decoration?"

He shouted his words, which is what you had to do to be heard over the roaring noise of the lunchroom. Birch Hills High had a closed campus, which meant the cafeteria was a cavernous former gymnasium with the atmosphere of a prison yard. Because we couldn't go to the fast food places, they came to us, paying a hefty rent to sell Pizza Hut and Taco Bell to a captive market. As much as it seemed creepily corporate, it was nice to have textbooks that postdated the fall of the Berlin Wall, which the school didn't until the fast food contracts came in.

"Fucked up," Li said. He'd found out about Apple Boy's fate through Kenzie. If there was one person who wasn't going to run his mouth about things, it was Li.

"I think it's called Grand Theft." I shrugged.

"*And* Receiving Stolen Goods, I guess," Erik added. "Pretty serious."

He dipped a French fry in catsup, and then used it to paint an inverted pentagram on the cinderblock wall beside us.

Our table was a conglomeration of freaks from across the spectrum of Birch Hills High. Besides Erik, Li, and me, there was Mike Kahuakai, an oversized Samoan freshman with a shaved head and hemp jewelry; a tall, albino kid named Richard but called "Pink Dick," who had eyes like a lab rat and long hair the color of corn silk; and Twitch, a shaky anime geek who wore shirts printed with dragons and lightning bolts. Together, we took up one of the smaller tables.

With Erik and Pink Dick around, almost nobody would say much to us. Pink Dick supposedly had buried a cat up to its neck and then ran it over with a lawnmower. He made a brand in the shape of a cross in metal shop and burned it (upside down) into his arm. People thought he was a certifiable psycho. I thought he was okay, but the thing about the cat really bothered me at first. After I got to know him a bit better, Pink Dick told me the cat thing was a story he and his older brother made up to freak out some girls at a softball game years ago. He was glad people believed it, though. I asked him why, and he said that it made everyone stop staring at him and asking him stupid questions about being an albino. When the cat rumor got out, nobody would even glance his way anymore. He said it was one of the best things to ever happen to him.

"Wanna go out to the Farm later tonight?" Erik asked me.

"Huh? Are you serious?" I'd thought after being held prisoner by a bunch of meth-heads, he'd stopped seeing the allure of that place.

"Yeah, why not? Pink Dick and I are going out there to jam."

"You can play as loud as you want," Dick said. "You play bass, right? You should bring it, too. They don't give a fuck."

"Yeah, I might. I might have plans, though," I said.

They gaped at me.

"What? I have a life, you know."

"Oh, yeah, you mean with Lindsay," Dick said. "I heard about that. You know she was probably just scamming that night, right?"

"What do you mean?" I said.

Erik nudged him, and he sneered.

"You should come along," Erik said. "You can ride with me."

Later, between classes, Lindsay floated through the hallway crowd and grabbed my arm. She was headed out to the Farm later and wanted to know if I'd be out there. Of course, I said "yes."

"You want us to pick you up on the way?" I asked, trying to look indifferent as I put some books in my backpack.

She tapped one her combat boots' toes on the floor. "I kinda already got a ride, and Erik's back seat is really small."

"Oh." I stood there looking stupidly down at my bright orange AP History book.

"But I'll see you out there," she added.

I shrugged, put the book in my backpack, and then zipped it up. With all my effort, I concealed a pout.

"Awww," she said, telling me I'd failed. "Don't worry. I like you."

She kissed my cheek and then darted away, the black tails of her trench coat trailing behind her. Her lips' warmth spread across my face and filled my body.

That night, I put my bass in its gig bag (I'd never actually had a "gig") and placed my 30-watt practice amp by the door. My mom told me how "exciting" it was that I had kept up with my musical interests and asked if I wanted to bring along the "extra cookies" from her last batch. It was at that point I decided to walk over to Erik's house with my gear rather than risk the possibility of her offering us Kool-Aid and cheese sandwiches when he came over.

Erik's dad opened the front door, which startled me a bit. His mom usually was the one who answered the bell.

"Well." He raised a glass of scotch, and then scratched at his impeccable gray beard. "Aren't you going to say 'trick-or-treat'?"

I shifted under the bass strapped on my back.

"I'm just having a bit of fun with you, sorry," he said. "Come on in."

I stepped into the foyer and closed the door behind me. The pink twilight sky glowed above the vaulted glass ceiling. Erik's dad strolled through the archway into the great room, hollering "Erik! Sid Vicious is here!" He looked back at me and asked, "That's a bass in there, right?"

"Uh-huh."

"Be down in a second," Erik yelled back, his voice echoing from the second floor.

"He'll be right down," Erik's dad said to me. He finished his scotch and ambled over to one of the leather couches. A fifth of Johnny Walker Black sat on the glass table, half-drained, and a huge projection TV tuned to CNN lit the room. "Come on in, make yourself at home."

"So, what's Mrs. Grundler up to these days?" I asked.

I suddenly felt self-conscious for asking, because I worried this might reveal to Erik's dad that that I had a crush on his wife. He chuckled.

"Not really my job to know, amigo, not tonight. And vice-versa for the lady." He refilled his glass. "You guys forming a band?"

"I dunno. I like punk. Erik likes metal."

"Creative differences. That breaks up the best bands, you know. That and hard drugs." He took off his Lennon glasses and rubbed his eyes. "Don't ever get into heroin."

"Yes, sir."

President Clinton's head filled the giant screen. The words *Impeachment Proceedings* were printed below it.

"Trying to ruin that man's life over a blowjob," Mr. Grundler snorted. "And Kissinger just walks around like nothing went down. Our country's priorities are fucked, kid."

Erik plodded down the stairs in a black Mayhem shirt and snow-print camouflage pants. He glanced over at the bottle and then rolled his eyes.

"Hello, Son," Mr. Grundler said, warmly. "I was just having a chat with your friend, here."

I realized Mr. Grundler didn't know my name.

"Not more goddamn hippie stories, I hope." Erik pulled on his leather jacket. "Dad used to hang out with the White Panthers and the MC5," he said to me.

"Really? You never told me that."

"Of course he didn't." Erik's dad sighed. "He doesn't care."

"Sure I do." Erik said. "I'll be back later, Dad. Love ya."

"Love you, too," he said, not looking away from the TV.

It wasn't until we got out to the Farm that I realized how insufficient my musical gear was. Erik played a black Gibson SG Gothic and had brought a Marshal twin. Pink Dick had a Peavey half-stack and a Paul Reed Smith seven-string. I had an off-brand 30-watt practice amp and a battered Japanese-made bass. When we set up in a semi-circle, my gear looked like the bottom of an evolutionary ladder. Kenzie came in as we were setting up in the pole barn, pointed at my equipment, and laughed.

"Nice," he said. "You pick that up at Bigmart on the way?"

"Shut up, Kenzie," I mumbled. "I bet I play better than you."

"'Cause I don't play. Bet I'm better at golf than you, though. Who gives a shit about bass players, anyway? Name a famous bass player."

"Geezer Butler," Erik chimed in as he adjusted his amp's knobs.

"Les Claypool," added Dick.

"Flea," I said.

Kenzie scoffed.

"Quite a bounty they got out for Apple Boy, eh?" Erik said.

"Ain't no Apple Boy here," Kenzie said. "But you should check this out."

He walked over the workbench, where a sheet draped over what I now recognized as a standing human shape.

"Say hello to my little friend. I give you…Captain Fiji!"

Kenzie pulled down the sheet, revealing what Apple Boy had become after just a couple days at the Farm. He wore a pair of mirrored aviator sunglasses, and his little hat had been swapped out for a frayed Tigers cap. A bright orange Hawaiian shirt printed with multicolored margaritas covered up his Victorian garb. A cigarette hung from his lips. The box of apples had been taken away, and now he held a beer in either hand. His shoes were gone. I laughed along with everyone else. The transformation was so complete that almost no remnant of Apple Boy remained.

"Wow," Erik said. "He's livin' it."

"Hells yeah," Kenzie said.

"Awesome," Dick cackled. "You should send a pic of this to the *Observer*."

"Yeah," Kenzie said. "But Jason's too paranoid, and he runs shit for Travis. And Trav, well, you know. Not much of a sense of humor."

"What's Captain Fiji the captain of?" I asked.

"He's captain of the motherfuckin' party, yo!" His smile crinkled the lines around his eyes. "Well, you dudes have fun. I'm gonna take off before you make me deaf with your shitty music."

We all flipped him off, and away he went.

After playing a few songs we all knew, we just jammed together, with Erik shouting out the key changes. They turned down so my bass wouldn't be totally drowned out, but the two of them were a lot better than me and seemed to have a real chemistry. It didn't bother me; I actually thought it was pretty cool. I took off my bass and leaned it on the amplifier.

"You done already?" Erik asked.

"Done, no, just taking a break. Besides, you two probably want to crank the volume." I jerked my head toward the door. "I'm going to see who else is up at the house."

Of course, I was hoping to find Lindsay. A wind came in off the fields, blowing trash across the snowy yard. I plodded up onto the back porch with my teeth chattering.

As soon as I stepped inside, Lindsay's laugh came from the front room, along with an indistinct male voice rumbling in response. The kitchen smelled like piss. Shotgun shells and blackened wads of foil lay strewn across the table. I stepped over a pile of cans and fast-food wrappers and made my way down the hall. What I saw when I turned the corner froze me to the bone.

Jason sat in a tattered recliner, with Annoying Amanda on his good knee. She stroked his broad chest, resting her head on his dreadlocks. He had one of his hands down the front of her pants, working like a digging crab. And then there was Lindsay.

She sat on the couch with René, who held a Bowie knife up to her face. I thought for a moment he was about to slice her cheek, but then I spotted the straw pinched like a cigarette between her black-nailed fingers. He was murmuring something in French, holding the big, broad knife flat, like a tray. A line of meth ran down the blade.

Lindsay's bony, bare knees pressed together, and she twisted the sole of one of her boots against the side of the other. Beside René, she looked terrifyingly small and unsure if she should laugh or scream. I turned to stone, watching this.

"Come on, baby." He took a sharp breath through his teeth. "You know what to do."

She looked away from him, finally noticing me in the room. Time flew back into motion. She gasped and sprung away from René, who cursed her, swinging back the knife, careful not to dump the line.

I bolted out the back door. All I could think of was getting away. The crunching of my shoes through the snow sounded strange, distorted, as I hurried toward the barn. Electric guitars wailed their dirge from inside. Lindsay scrambled after me.

"Please listen," she pleaded, putting her hand on my shoulder. "They told me you guys weren't coming. Then I saw Erik's car, and they said you'd all left with Kenzie. I swear."

I stopped and turned. She was out of breath and not wearing her coat.

"Is that what you want to do?" I asked. "That in there?"

"No. Amanda's the one who likes Jason. I just didn't want her to come out here alone. They told me you guys were gone, and then it started to get all weird."

"Why didn't you leave, then? Huh?"

"Because I thought trying to leave would make it even worse. Did you see that fucking knife? Amanda's truck is broken down again. Neither of us had a ride, and I didn't know anyone else was out here." She shivered. "Sometimes it's just safer to do what guys want. At least it doesn't make it worse."

She came over and hugged me. It was as if she was trying to force her body inside my own.

"Promise me," I said, "that you won't do that with them."

"I promise," she whispered. "Can we just get Amanda and get the fuck out of here?"

"Yeah, sure," I said. "Let's grab Erik."

"You get him," she said. "I'll see if I can get her out of there."

Erik was alright with cutting their jam short. I helped load his amplifier into his trunk. Lindsay came out with her black, fake-leather riding coat on, shaking her head.

"She doesn't want to leave," she said.

"Crap." I looked to Erik. "What should we do?"

He shrugged.

"We should go," Lindsay said. "It's what she wants."

"We can't do that," I said.

I didn't like Amanda, but I sure didn't feel good about stranding her at the Farm with two huge meth-heads and one very large knife.

"Jesus, Josh," Erik said. "She wants to get fucked up and laid. Maybe by both of them. Let it go."

Lindsay put her hand on the small of my back, and said, "It's fine."

I said, "No, it isn't. Not really."

But I got into the car with everyone else and left Amanda there, anyway. We all went to the waffle place to drink coffee and play euchre. With Lindsay next to me, I couldn't keep myself from glancing over at the scars running up her forearms like little white ladders with crooked rungs. I wondered what they led to and where they came from.

"You think Amanda will be okay?" I asked.

"It's her life," Lindsay said. "She's used to it."

She tore the corner off a packet of artificial sweetener, poured it onto her tongue, and swallowed.

8

The day after Christmas brought a sense of desperation. Once the feast had denigrated to the status of leftovers, after every holiday classic had been re-run on TV for the thousandth time, when the wrapping paper had been cleared away, the reunited family ceased to be a novelty and there wasn't much holiday spirit left. The secret sentimental joy I felt when we all decorated the Christmas tree now turned to a dread of the inevitable re-packing. Every bulb and candy cane was a campaign sign the day after the election—just another clean-up on the horizon.

My brother, Paul, had been home from college for over a week. At first, I'd been thrilled to see him. We argued about whether *Dark City* was better than *The Crow*, took turns on the Playstation, and went to the comic book shop. But soon, the cracks started to show. He complained about my music. His quiet bookishness had turned into a haughty expertise on everything. He'd also become a Libertarian, which became a major talking point of his to everyone in the family. I suppose it was a logical progression after being an obsessive *Star Trek* fan, but it was tedious as hell.

Once, when going off about the rights of unfettered commerce and the duty of every individual to live up to his full potential, Dad finally told him, "I hope this is a phase. Every young Republican who reads Ayn Rand ends up calling himself a Libertarian at some point. I raised you to have a better heart than that."

Paul turned a deep pink and lowered his head. We all went back to watching *A Charlie Brown Christmas*, and nothing more was said about it.

It was the only thing anyone had said to him about his new politics that didn't fuel his arguments. As much as I hated to have the Catholic shame-hammer dropped on me, it was nice to see someone shut him up. By the day after Christmas, I could hardly stand to be in the house anymore.

One of the many reasons was that I was so horny I thought I might spontaneously combust. If I couldn't jerk off at least two or three times a day, I couldn't think straight. I never felt guilty after doing it. Instead, I felt a sudden Zen-like clarity of vision and purpose after the haze of orgasm passed. I felt like a normal person again. Without these releases, I felt like a freak; while watching *It's a Wonderful Life* with my parents, I'd imagined myself doing depraved things to Donna Reed. It was awful.

It was hard enough to clear out my urges when I had a chatty mom, a little sister, and an insomniac dad. Add a brother back into the mix, and I was screwed. The long hours between shower time and bed were more than I could bear. (No way could I do it in the bathroom, with Mom's Maxipads in the trash and my little sister watching *Sailor Moon* in the next room. My bedroom door had no lock either, and knocking was unheard of at home.) So, that's how I ended up heading out to see the hot tub lady.

On the far side of Whispering Meadows subdivision stood a marsh and some woods that were saved from development because of their wetlands status. A few trails led through this area, past elms and maples, around abandoned campers and rusty car frames covered with grape ivy. On the other side, a bluff overlooked Manor Estates Trailer Park. Just beyond that stretched the expressway, with its endless roar of traffic going east-west at all hours. It was surreal, the difference between neighborhoods on each side of the wilds. Row after row of dilapidated trailers and cluttered yards stretched out beneath the ridge, their trashcans curbside all week long, their satellite dishes like gray blossoms looking heavenward, the jacked-up trucks and crumbling muscle cars catching the sun like scattered toys. From up on the slope, one could easily see down into the backyards. Especially with a pair of binoculars. Which is how I'd found the hot tub lady the summer before.

Honestly, I'd been bird watching. We've always had a bird feeder at our house, and spotting birds has been a hobby of mine for as long as I can remember. Like a lot of things, it was something I was really into for a short period, and then I kind of lost interest, but I returned to it now and then. I was looking for hawks, actually, but didn't find any. Just the normal blue jays, mourning doves, and cardinals. Disheartened, I'd come out on the slope. I was bored and alone, so I lay down on my belly and looked down at the trailer park with my binoculars, imagining I was a commando surveying an enemy encampment.

My gaze swung past a backyard just as a woman wrapped in a beach towel emerged from the back door of her doublewide. My vision bounced wildly as I swept the binoculars back to follow her. She stepped down from the deck and walked toward a hot tub. A high plank fence had been built around the backyard, as well as several tall bushes. I suppose she figured no one could see in. She dropped the towel, revealing her voluptuous middle-aged figure. She had hips like an Amazon warrior on the cover of a fantasy paperback and the breasts to match. The sun had bronzed the whole of her deep sienna, deepening her saucer-sized nipples to the color of chocolate. Her ratty black hair had been teased up into a storm cloud, the same shade as the thatch between her legs.

It didn't occur to me that what I was doing was wrong, or invasive, or, even perhaps, pervy. Even if it had, it was as if I'd spotted a phoenix exploding in a column of rainbow flames. I couldn't have looked away if I tried.

Of course, after this, numerous other bird watching trips through the woods ended up on that bluff. Enough times that I figured out the hot tub lady took a dip almost every day at around seven o'clock, year round, unless her husband was home from his truck route. Whenever the semi cab was parked on the street out front, she wore a swimsuit to bathe. She and her husband would both sit in the tub, facing each other but not touching. With his thick moustache and stocky body, he looked a bit like how I imagined woodsmen in fairytales. I never watched the two of them together—that felt too weird. If the big rig was parked out front, I always just strolled back home.

At six-thirty on the day after Christmas, as my family gathered around a jigsaw puzzle, I snuck off to go "on a hike." Trudging through the snow like a Mountie on patrol, I finally emerged from the woods. The wintertime didn't offer tall grass and leafy trees for cover, so I was pretty much limited to crouching in a stand of pines on the hill, peering through my binoculars.

The truck wasn't parked out front, a good sign. Then I realized that maybe the hot tub lady and her husband were visiting relatives somewhere. Or maybe she didn't work her regular shift over the holidays, throwing off her bathing schedule. After ten agonizing minutes of waiting, the trailer's back door opened and she stepped out, wearing only her towel.

But she wasn't alone. A skinny guy with a potbelly and a close-cut beard followed, also wearing only a towel. It wasn't her husband. He looked familiar.

The two of them hurried through the snow to the hot tub in long, goofy steps, laughing. They folded back the tub's cover, dropped their towels, and jumped naked into the steaming cauldron. As soon as they embraced, I recognized the man. It took me a moment to place him without his glasses, naked, in the trailer park.

It was Erik's dad, Mr. Grundler.

I liked Mrs. Grundler. And even though he was weird, Mr. Grundler seemed nice enough, too. I also liked, in my own perverted Peeping Tom way, the hot tub lady. I didn't know what to make of any of this.

I considered that maybe, just maybe, it was some sort of platonic, non-sexual, naked hot tubbing occurring between mature adults. That theory was dashed when he lifted himself to sit on the edge of the tub, his cock hard and pink, and the hot tub lady started to blow him. My stomach twisted like a wrung washcloth. I lowered my binoculars and started back home.

My pent-up libido had evaporated like the Jacuzzi water steaming from Mr. Grundler's bare thighs. I walked back on the streets rather than though the woods, passing thousands of colored lights burning in celebration of a day that had already passed.

When I got home, there was a battered Ford Taurus parked in our driveway. One of Paul's old high school friends, I assumed. Dejected and a bit freaked out my voyeuristic misadventure, I carefully placed my boots on the plastic mat just inside the door, stowed my binoculars in the closet, and hung up my coat. I walked into the kitchen to find everyone gathered around the half-finished jigsaw puzzle on the table.

Lindsay Kruthers was sitting in the chair usually reserved for me. With her fishnet arm-warmers and Wednesday Addams dress, she looked like a blot of black ink on an otherwise Kodak-moment family scene. She must have seen the look of surprise on my face, because she instantly said, "Boo!"

Mom, Dad, Alison, and Paul all looked over at me. My brother smirked.

"Hey, Lindsay." I rubbed the back of my neck, wondering if things could get much weirder. "What's going on?"

"Your mom said I could come in and wait for you to get back from your hike," she said.

"She put together that part of the sky," Alison said, pointing at the puzzle. A fractured sunset hung half-assembled over a mostly-formed lighthouse.

"That's right." Mom smiled.

Lindsay stood up, saying, "Let me show you my new car," then to my family, "It was nice meeting you."

After some more pleasantries, my brother and Dad exchanged looks as I turned to follow her. I pulled on my coat and boots again, and we walked out.

"Well, that's my car," she said, gesturing to the burgundy Taurus. "I got it from my older sister, of all people. My mom only let me keep it so I can get a job."

"Where's your sister?"

"Seattle," she said. "Took off, like, five years ago, haven't seen her since. But she writes and calls pretty regular."

I nodded. I wasn't quite sure how her sister got a car from Seattle to Birch Hills without driving it there but let it go.

"Want to go for a ride?" she asked.

"Where to?" I asked.

"You'll see," Lindsay said. "Come on."

So I got in the car with her. She pointed at the tape deck.

"Check out my cutting-edge stereo," she said. "There's a box of my sister's old tapes by your feet."

I dug through the shoebox of cassettes as she backed out of the driveway. Metallica's *Load* album, Ted Nugent, Motley Crue, Poison. Slim pickings. I settled on Motorhead's *Bastards*.

"So," she said as she turned onto Edgemoor Drive, "is that the sort of thing your family usually does?"

"What do you mean?"

"You know, do jigsaw puzzles together and drink cocoa?"

"No," I said. "Well, yeah, kind of." I looked out at the black woods. "I know it's lame."

"No, it's not," she said. "My sister ran away, my dad's an ex-con, and my mom's a psycho Jesus bitch. *That's* lame. Really lame."

"What's your mom's religion?"

"You know the mom in the movie *Carrie*?"

"I'm sure she means well."

"I want to beat her to death," she said, "with a shovel."

"How was your Christmas, then?"

"It was okay. I got a car."

"I wish I did."

When we turned off of Edgemoor and started to head toward the boonies, unease scurried down my back.

"You're not taking me out to the Farm, are you?"

She glanced over. "Maybe. Don't worry, I have your Christmas present there. You'll like it."

"I will?"

She nodded.

"I can't believe we're going out to the Farm," I said as we passed a bullet-riddled NO HUNTING sign. "It's like Tatooine."

"Tattooing?"

"Tatooine. The desert planet in *Star Wars*. It's this out-of-the-way, crappy sand planet run by a Mafioso space-slug, but everybody in the series goes there. And I'm always like, if this place is such an unimportant backwater hellhole, why is it in almost all the *Star Wars* movies?"

I realized I'd probably just gone a bit too far on the geek train, because she didn't say anything at first. But then, when the tape clicked and flipped over, she spoke.

"It's where they're from," she said.

"Huh?"

"The Skywalkers. They're from that desert place, right? The one with that bar and all the aliens."

"Yeah," I said. "I mean, they grew up there."

"Well, that's why they keep going back to it."

We pulled into the driveway at the Farm. Amanda's face peeked out the front window. She waved at Lindsay and laughed.

"Come on out to the barn with me."

Lindsay pulled a duffle bag out of the back seat and slung it over her shoulder. She took me by the hand, and I followed.

She closed the barn door behind us and then wedged it shut with a plank. The diminutive Apple Boy/Captain Fiji stood at attention on the workbench across the barn. One of his beers had been swapped out for a giant foam finger, the kind you get at sporting events with "Number 1!" printed on it. He held it up in a frozen cheer.

Lindsay walked to the packed dirt floor's center, dropped the duffle bag and shrugged off her coat. She opened up her arms, wide. I ran to her.

The moment Lindsay was within reach, she took two sudden steps backward. Her arms rose, crossing at the wrists, in front of her breasts. She held her palms out to push me away. Hunched in the shadow of one of the barn's overhead beams, she looked through me, focused on something beyond the present moment or place. My hand hovered between us like something inappropriate.

The first syllable of a word I hadn't chosen yet came from my throat as a quick apologetic sound. She greeted it with a faint smile. I squared my shoulders, and Lindsay skipped forward. She pulled my hand toward her, reaching behind herself to wrap my arm around her waist. Her cheek pressed into my collarbone as we held ourselves against one another.

"Merry Christmas." She took a deep lazy breath, nuzzling her cheek against my shoulder, and said, "I like you."

"I," I stammered back the stronger word, "I like you, too, Linds."

She pressed her hips against me to lean back at the waist and look in my eyes. I'd spent untold hours remembering her face when I was alone and longing, walking in the woods or curled up with blankets over my head, imagining what it might be like to be in a situation like this. I felt kind of ashamed. Someone from classroom daydreams and bathroom jerk-offs stood holding me as an actuality, smelling faintly of vanilla, smoke, and laundry soap, seeing me at the same time as I saw her. I bowed my head. Lindsay reached up, took off my glasses, and slipped them into her purse.

Our lips met and mouths opened. It wasn't like the first time we kissed, when her tongue was frantic and insistent, her mouth a mire of whiskey as she gripped me the base of my skull. The tips of our tongues gently touched. We shared our breath and the taste of hot chocolate.

Outside, the wind whistled and muttered against the barn, and the only other sounds were our clothes rustling, our feet shifting, and our mouths wordlessly moving together. It was unspoken and understood, and for once, I wasn't worried how it might end.

She wasn't my first. I'd bent wrists and cramped hands reaching down pants or up skirts. I had my share of sour beer kisses by bonfires or sloppy oral in basements, usually with pounding music and often with prying eyes. But this time, Li wouldn't open the closet looking for his hat and find me being rubbed raw by some girl from the subdivision one mile over. This time, my fingers wouldn't get caught in a banana hair-clip like it did with Sara Schwarz, I wouldn't cum underwater from Amy Golding rubbing her thick ass against me night-swimming, I wouldn't lose the condom, I wouldn't be asked "Are you sure you've done this before?" I wouldn't say something to make her laugh when I didn't mean to, like, "Does this mean I'm your boyfriend now?"

This time, I wasn't trembling—or at least not with fear.

Her kisses on my neck turned into quick, sharp bites, urging me on as my hands plucked open her dress's buttons. It fell open, revealing her bra as black lace triangles, so stark against her that they seemed stenciled onto her skin. Kissing her shoulder, I looped my thumb inside one of the cups. Had I trimmed my nails lately? I pulled the fabric down to reveal a pink nipple ringed by goose bumps. Her grip tightened on my shoulders as I pulled it into my mouth. She bit down on my neck and, when I tensed, moved to sigh in my ear, rubbing her palm in slow circles on my hard-on. Gently, she pulled my hand to the coolness of her bare thigh. Her other hand slowed on my cock, pressing down in long strokes. She led my fingers up between her thighs, placing them on the naked heat between her legs. She tensed in my arms, and I don't know if she pulled away or if only the moment did. My hands dropped to my sides, and I searched her face.

"It's okay," she said. "But, Jesus, your hands are fucking freezing."

"I left my gloves in my other coat," I stammered.

She laughed when I cupped my hands over my mouth and blew, trying to warm them. Lindsay knelt down and unzipped the duffle bag to unpack a couple blankets and some condoms. We laid out the blankets, each taking a corner and draping them over the packed dirt. I struggled out of my boots and then the rest of my clothes. I left my socks and underwear on. She slipped out of her dress and bra, and my eyes drank in the surprise of her body. It wasn't the silvery scars across her arms and thighs, or her thinness, but rather her fullness that surprised me. Her apple-sized breasts stood pert and round, the tiniest webs of blue radiating around their nipples. A small constellation of acne stood pink and angry between them on the triangle of breastbone. Her latticed ribcage formed an arch over her belly's smoothness. A silver bead jutted above her navel to hold the purple gem glinting in its hollow. Her ass and thighs carried an incongruent heaviness; the dramatic flare of her hips framed her pussy, shaved bare, so much more beautiful and elegant than what now throbbed in my tighty-whitey underwear. She'd left on her thigh-high stockings, stripes of black-and-white ringing her narrow legs. With her fire-orange hair, green eyes, and the gooseflesh rippling over her pale body's scars, every inch of her was goddess-like yet human, tough yet vulnerable—and I, standing in my socks with a boner-tent, felt ridiculous.

"Get in here, and *please* take those off," she laughed out, kneeling down and sliding between the blankets.

I obeyed, and we lay down together. She went down on me until my back arched, and I pulled her away, gasping that I didn't want to yet, and then I did the same for her as she cooed, coached, and warned, the soles of her feet rubbing on my hips and back. She reached for the condom and opened it as I did this, and then her long fingers guided me up and onto my back just as my jaw began to ache. She slid the condom on me with an ease that brought the ugly thought of how many times she had done this before, and with whom. I forced the thought away by looking up at her straddling me, the thick blanket draped over her shoulders like a priestess's cloak. Warmth consumed us as she reached down to guide me, wincing once before shifting her hips and pressing them down to take me inside.

She placed her hands on my chest and threw her head back. A trickle of her wetness trailed down the inside of my thigh. I gripped her hip with one hand, caressing her with the other. Our breath quickened in time with the undulations of our bodies. A throbbing ache of pleasure built when she leaned forward to suck on my tongue and give hungry kisses.

I tried to calm myself, struggling to remember the order of the Presidents. George Washington. John Adams. Thomas Jefferson. Lindsay cooed and gasped, reaching back to stroke my scrotum as she mounted me. A spasm of ecstasy. I groaned and shifted beneath her.

My brain shouted, *Andrew Jackson.*

No, wrong. Way too soon for Old Hickory. James Madison? Or was it Monroe? The other Adams. She bit my ribs then trailed her mouth up to my neck. Harrison, goddammit, when was William Henry Harrison?

I clenched my teeth, sweat cooling on my brow, and switched

tactics, thinking of all the different Green Lanterns. Alan Scott. Hal Jordan. Guy Gardner.

"Good, baby, relax. It's good," she sighed.

Galius Zed, who fought Grayven, the third son of Darkseid. Kyle Rainer. Arisia Rrab, named by the writers after the planet Arisia in the Lensman novels by E. E. "Doc" Smith: *The Grey Lensman, Children of the Lens.*

I touched her face. She sucked my pinky into her mouth. Her hand worked down between her thighs.

Kilowog, from Sector 674. Sinestro, who had been Jordan's mentor, but he turned evil. He had to. His name was "Sinestro."

"Fuck," she squeaked.

And then I was there, wholly and totally. Orgasm swept over me like a wave, and then receded as cold fire when I came. I stayed hard, though, and sat up with Lindsay still wrapped and rocking against me, kissing her face and shoulders as she rhythmically cried until she grabbed me and tightened her hands on my throat, her body tensing and then unwinding in a long, shuddering sigh. I held her, drained, rapturous, with the vague worry I might never think about the Green Lantern in the same way ever again.

Afterward, we huddled between blankets. There wasn't any heat in the barn, and my sweat turned to feverish chills.

"Linds?"

"Huh?"

"Why do you cut yourself?"

"Wow, nice post-sex chat, baby. Why ask that?"

"I'm sorry," I said. "I just want to know about you."

"I dunno." A divot formed between her eyebrows and she frowned, thinking. "For the high, I guess. Or when I can't deal with stuff hurting so bad, it sort of pushes the reset button on my brain." She nuzzled against me. "That, and maybe I just like the taste of blood."

"What hurts you so bad that you'd want to do that?"

She stared up at the ceiling, not looking at me. "You wouldn't get it."

"Try me," I said. "I want to—"

She pressed a finger to my lips. "Don't you dare say you want to help me."

A bang on the door jerked us both into sitting positions.

"Lindsay," Amanda called from the other side. "Get dressed and unlock the door. Jason's gonna be out here, and he's pissed."

We dressed in a panic. Lindsay opened the door as I struggled to stuff the blankets back in the bag. Amanda came in, looking shaken. One side of her face was pink and puffy. I was sure she'd been slapped.

"Cops just showed up, but they left," Amanda said. "We gotta clear this place out before they come back."

"They looking for drugs?" Lindsay said, pulling on her coat. "Guns? The chopped cars?"

"Statutory rape?" I offered. "Domestic abuse?"

Amanda shot me a look.

"No." She pointed across the barn, at Captain Fiji. "They're looking for him."

I laughed. I couldn't help it. With all of the shit going on at the Farm, what brought the sheriff out was the theft of a holiday ornament from the park in Birch Hills. Not the drugs, or the guns, not the fighting and underage drinking and sex. A robotic street urchin's welfare was more valued than anyone else's out here.

Jason roared outside as he made his way to the barn, "Get it the *fuck* out of here."

The door flew open and he barged in, his cane tip ramming against the ground with every step. Kenzie followed him, and René leaned in the doorframe. Jason glared at Lindsay, Amanda, and me, and then punched one of the standing beams. I jumped.

"What the hell?" Jason closed and opened his fist, which now bled from the knuckles. "Is this place a playground?"

I considered saying if he thought of Amanda as a child after what he was doing with her, he'd better not take any babysitting jobs. I decided he'd stomp me to death, though.

"Dude, chill," Kenzie said. "I mean, if they knew he was here, they would've busted in and taken him."

"I don't fucking care. Your stupid prank got the cops at our door. You think I'm going to risk going back to the joint for *this*?"

"The man, he has a point," René said. "I say to Kenzie at the time—"

"Shut up, you French twat," Jason said. "You helped make this mess. I need him gone. Fucking gone in an hour. I mean where no one will find him ever again. Do it. I'll take care of the rest of the shit around here. You better pray that Travis doesn't hear about this."

Jason strode off, and Amanda followed him.

"But J-boy," Kenzie called after him. "Fiji is the Captain of the Party!"

"What a very rude man," René said. "We must bury him, Kenzie."

"Oh, that's a bit harsh," Kenzie said. "Jason can be a real asshole, but I don't think I'm cool with that."

Lindsay giggled. I poked her.

"Not Jason, you dumb shit," he said. "Mr. Fiji, here."

"Captain Fiji," I corrected.

"That's right." Kenzie pointed at me. "I hope you realize how—" He trailed off, sucking in his lips and taking a breath. "This is wrong. I don't think I can go through with it. Captain Fiji didn't do anything to deserve this."

Deserve, of course, had nothing to do with it.

"We'll help you," Lindsay said. "We'll help you take care of him."

"The party's over, dude," Kenzie said to the animatronic boy. He turned to us and asked, "Could I have a minute to myself here?"

We closed the door behind us when we walked out. Stars throbbed in the sky, and the snow sparkled like broken glass.

"I don't know why I feel bad for that guy, but I do. He seems alright." She lit a smoke and said, "I didn't mean to get us dragged into this."

"It's okay. Totally worth it," I said. "Next time, though, let's get a motel room."

"Ew." She scrunched up her nose. "Isn't that kinda skanky?"

"Worse than a meth dealer's unheated barn?"

"I guess you got a point." She looked down.

Jason and Amanda yelled at each other inside the house. Out on the back porch, René talked in a hushed voice on his phone, sticking a finger in his other ear. He gave the two of us a long glare as we crossed the yard.

"I didn't know where else to take you," she said, pulling the Russian hat out of her ammo-bag purse. "I'm sorry."

"No, I didn't mean—look, it's fine. Let's go get some coffee from the gas station, then come back to help get rid of Apple Boy-Fiji-whoever."

"That'd be good."

She shivered and pulled on her hat. I looped my arm around her waist, and she leaned against me as we ambled toward the driveway. Erik's car had appeared, parked behind Lindsay's Taurus. The front storm door banged, and he hurried toward the Acura with a garbage sack slung over his shoulder, Santa-style. He froze when he saw us.

"How'd you guys get out here?" He wavered on his feet a bit, gawking from beneath a black knit hat with the word "DOWN" in gothic letters across its brow.

"I got a car," Lindsay said, with some pride. "You get anything good for Christmas?"

"A DVD player."

He darted over to his car, set down the bag, and opened his trunk. His right hand was heavily bandaged. As he set the bag inside, he asked, "What are you guys up to?"

"We did it in the pole barn," she said. "And now we're going to get some coffee."

He locked his trunk and said, "Sounds fun. I'm gonna be here for a bit. I'll move the car so you can get out."

"We'll be back," I said.

Her Taurus's cabin was still warm when Lindsay and I drove away. Detroit rock radio crackled out some familiar song I never actually listened to. Like a drowsy cat, I stretched out in the passenger seat. My left hand gently curled around her thigh, under her dress, warming the smooth skin between her stocking and panties. She widened her knees a bit before reaching over to squeeze my hipbone. I breathed deeply through my nose, taking in vanilla lotion and sharp sweat, the must of damp clothes and the musk of our bodies. I stiffened. My hand crept up her leg, my ring and pinky fingers rubbed against her moistened warmth. Her hips pressed back. The roads were empty. They seemed to have been built just for us.

The Oasis Truck Stop squatted on the frozen moonscape beside the interstate. Its sign could be seen from a mile away, a red-and-yellow planet hanging low in the sky. Rows of semis sat out back, slumbering machines housing men sleeping far from home. Lindsay's hand was warm in mine as we walked in easy lockstep through the doors. An electric chime caused the bulldog-faced woman behind the register to look up and smile before returning to her celebrity magazine. The coffee machine stood in the far corner beside stand-up coolers stocked with a rainbow of pop bottles. The same station we listened to in the car played inside. The deejay said the Doors were up next, and then a commercial for a bail bondsman played.

"Oh. My. God," Lindsay said, pulling me toward the gift section. "Look at these things."

The top shelf displayed huge plastic geode crystals in red, purple, and blue. Mounted on top of each was a different glass animal about the size of my hand: a unicorn, an eagle, a dolphin, and a bear. Individual boxes, labeled "Maji-Krystal Kreations," crowded the shelves below.

"Now that's what I call art," I said, standing behind her.

"I know, right?" She giggled and leaned back against me. "When I was little, I would have died for this." She pointed at the glass unicorn.

"Do you want it? I'll get it for you."

"No." She nuzzled my shoulder. "But that's sweet, though."

"I'd get you all of the glass unicorns in the world." I slid my hands into her trench coat pockets. "You're beautiful. You're a Maji-Krystal Kreation." I kissed her neck below the earlobe.

"No, you are," she sighed. "You're the Maji-Krystal-ist ever."

We walked down the aisles, me behind her with my hands in her pockets, cooing nonsense about magic crystals and glass unicorns, until we reached the crappachino machine and each filled up a big Styrofoam cup with hazelnut. I paid for them, and the old woman behind the counter winked at me. As the Oasis Truck Stop's fluorescent glare faded in the rearview on our return trip, and Lindsay said, "You're lucky to have a friend like Erik. He's a pretty cool guy."

"What do you mean?"

"You two seem really close, that's all."

"Yeah." I slurped my coffee and looked out at the starlit fields rushing by. "I feel like there are a lot of things he doesn't tell me about, though."

"And I suppose you tell him absolutely everything, right? Everybody has to have some secrets."

The memory of what I'd seen Erik's dad doing earlier that night lurched in my bowels like bad meat, but I didn't say anything.

By the time we got back to the Farm, arrangements had been made. Captain Fiji's funeral group moved in two vehicles down the dark, country roads. Kenzie and René rode in the truck carrying the body. Erik drove Lindsay and me.

"What's with the bag in the trunk?" I asked.

"A whole sack of none-of-your-business." He fiddled with the car stereo, struggling due to the bandages.

"What happened to your hand?" I asked.

"This twenty questions? Jesus. I punched a mirror." His voice was flat. "I punched a mirror, and it cut open my knuckles. I was in the ER forever."

"Can you still play guitar?" Lindsay asked.

"Not right now, no, but in a few weeks, it'll be fine."

"Why'd you do it?" I asked.

He coasted up to a stop sign and said, "I don't know." As the car sped up again, he said, "The next seven years are going to totally suck."

Getting rid of the ex-caroler proved to be an undertaking. The ground was frozen, so burial was out of the question. We drove to a huge, marshy pond on some state land about five miles from the Farm. By the truck's headlights, Kenzie and René busted open the ice with axes. Erik and I dragged Captain Fiji out to the hole, along with the tire chained to his feet. It wasn't easy.

Kenzie, sweaty and panting, threw his axe to the side. He pulled out his flask and took a long pull. The guy looked about ten years older tonight, tired and graying. Drunk. He stared down at the shrouded form of Captain Fiji and then over to the group of us, stammering out, "Shouldn't somebody, I don't know, say something?"

I wanted to say something like this:

"He was named Apple Boy by society, but called Captain Fiji by his friends. He walked between two worlds, rejoicing in both but belonging in neither. Some might say Apple Boy was only a child corrupted by wicked forces, that the office of Captain Fiji was one forced upon him. Others will say that he escaped a life of pantomimed goodness and lip-synced hymns, but this freedom was short-lived; the light that burns twice as bright burns half as long. Some might say he was just another freak, and he had it coming. All we know is that he lived, that he died, and he brought joy to some who knew him."

But that's not what I said. I didn't say anything. My mind was overloaded with thoughts of love, sex, death, and treachery. I could only hold Lindsay's hand, gazing at the light on the snow and our long shadows cast by the headlights' glare.

Erik sparked a joint and took a hit, holding it between the thumb and forefinger of his bandaged hand, and then he said, "I wonder who's next?"

René, standing with an axe on his shoulder, laughed. He kicked the sheet-wrapped thing into the water. It sank in the space of a breath.

9

Mrs. Gomez was a squat and bug-eyed art teacher with lipstick on her teeth. As the students filtered in, her voice came in rushed bursts, in between which she took huge gasps of air.

"Okay, everyone go to the racks and get your projects and return to your workstations for attendance and then please come to me if you need to use an X-acto so I can get your name on the sign-out sheet and you all can keep progressing on your wonderful artwork." *Gasp.* "I'm really pleased with how things are coming along, but some of you are a bit behind, so please remember we will be spraying them in two weeks."

Pink Dick slouched his way across the room with his half-finished plaster sculpture, an Egyptian-style cat he was copying out of a book. I wondered if he planned to cut its head off afterward. I was sculpting a rabbit, because I'd re-read *Watership Down* over break, and Lindsay had begun the figure from Munch's Scream. She sat hunched over a small paperback *Book of Questions*, her hair hiding her face, the roots forming a brownish stripe down the center of her head.

She read aloud, "Would you want to experience a year of perfect happiness if, at its end, you'd have no memory of it? If no, why not?"

"That's a stupid question." Dick took a seat across from us. "What difference does it make?"

"Yes or no," she said.

"He's right," I said. "If it were followed by a year of total sadness, I'd have to think about it. But if you just forget it, then it's just nothing."

"You guys suck." She flipped a few pages and then asked without looking up, "Do you think the world will be better or worse in one hundred years?"

"Stupid," Dick said. "There won't be a world left by then."

"You really think so?" I asked him.

He gave me a long, pitying look before pulling his hair back into a ponytail.

She flipped a page. "Would you rather have your goodness rewarded with love or money?"

"Goodness?" Dick said.

"I could use some money," I said. "I'm happy with the love I got."

Lindsay dropped the book into her purse before slipping her hand onto my thigh. I gave her a playful glare as she stroked up and down. She was trying to make me hard so I wouldn't be able to get up and use the sign out sheet after attendance.

"What's the matter, teapot? Why you squirming?"

I felt my cheeks flush, and Lindsay beamed.

"Okay, people, it's time for attendance," Mrs. Gomez called. "Some of you are lagging a bit behind—"

Li wandered into the room, wearing a puffy coat with his hair spiked. He sat next to Dick, reeking like a bong-rip.

"Thomas Li," Gomez chirped.

"Sup?"

"One more tardy will earn you a detention, Mr. Li." She made a mark on her attendance sheet.

Lindsay and I had both taken Art II as our elective for the second semester, our first class together in all of our years in Birch Hills. After it, we'd duck into the side hallway by east wing for a frenzied five-minute make out before she slipped a note into my sweaty palm and hurried off to her Spanish class. My senior year had become an endless cycle of tedium, anxiety, and longing broken up by bursts of erotic excitement.

Lindsay's mom had given up trying to keep track of her, but she maintained draconian rules under her roof. One of them was that no boys were allowed over, but she worked a swing shift late into the evening every other Thursday. On those days, Lindsay and I would walk to her house after school and then lay around her bedroom until dinnertime. Her room smelled like detergent and sandalwood. Messy stacks of vampire novels sat on her dresser beside a crowd of saint candles: glass cylinders filled with colored wax, each with a gaudy picture of Lazarus, Michael, Peter, or Jude. The first time I sat down on her canopied bed, I looked over at the dresser and said, "I didn't know you guys were Catholic." She laughed, as though it were the funniest thing she'd ever heard.

One Thursday after school, we dyed my hair from green to purple in her bathroom. It was a disaster, really. I ended up with a bunch of dark blotches down the back of my neck and spine, and we stained the floor, the sink, even part of the wall. Frantic, we scrubbed the crime scene with bleach and cleanser, and then went back to her room.

"It's the purplest thing ever," I said, sitting at the dressing table's mirror and taking in the dye job. I didn't think I was exaggerating. My head looked like a Day-Glo Muppet. I was still shirtless from the dying process, and the new color gave my skin a peachy pall. I looked alien.

"It looks awesome," she said. "God, look at your eyes. They look so blue now. You should wear eyeliner, too."

I snorted. "After all the shit I got from saying I'd sleep with Li if he were a girl, you want me to wear makeup? Why not a dress, too?"

"Just a sec." She grabbed the ammo-bag off the bed and desperately rifled around in it until she found a whittled-down eyeliner pencil. "Here. Turn and face me."

"Linds, no, come on."

"We'll take it off before we go out. Just let me see. Turn around."

I sighed and turned around on the stool, facing her with my back to the dressing table. She leaned forward and uncapped the pencil. After scolding me for flinching, she began to outline my eyes, one hand holding the lids between her thumb and forefinger, the other making quick little strokes with the pencil.

"My sister and I used to do each other's makeup. At the same time, we tried to do what the other was doing—hey, don't move." She stood back and folded her arms, looking at her work. "Now I'll have to make it thicker. Anyway, we got pretty good at it. Like a mirror game, being each other's reflections. My dad saw us doing it once, and he called us a couple of monkeys."

"That's kind of mean."

"No, it wasn't like that. He was laughing. Like monkey see, monkey do, I guess. He had some problems, yeah, but mostly with my mom." She hissed. "Hold still. Jesus, you'll lose an eye."

"Eye patches are cool," I said.

"Yeah. But then you'll have to get a parrot, and I hate 'em." She started on the other eye.

"They fought a lot?"

"After dad lost his Ford job, he just didn't do much other than sit around the house, and Mom would always bitch at him, so he'd go to the bar, and come back late, and then they'd fight about that—"

"I remember when they closed the Wixom plant."

"Yeah, but that wasn't us. He just quit. Saw a dude get his arm chopped off by one of the presses. Like, he'd seen things like that happen before, but that last time, I don't know. He woke up scared the next day. He just couldn't go back. He wrote me from jail a couple times and told me that in a letter."

"I'm sorry," I said.

"I'm just talking, not bleedin' my heart out here."

"What did he do?"

"Had an accident. Drove out of a bar parking lot and hit a kid on a bike with his truck. Got twelve years."

"That's what Jason did, sorta. He only did like five."

"Yeah, well, this was a kid he hit, and my dad wasn't some college football star. Cops had come by for him a few times before he went away. That's why Mom's wearing sunglasses in that picture with me and my sister in the living room. She had a black eye."

"You ever visit him?"

"He got out three years ago. Early. I don't know where he is now."

I didn't know what to say. I tried not to blink. "You must be glad he's gone."

"I'm glad that kind of shit's not going on anymore, but now Mom's just full-blown nuts. I know she has to work all the time, but the God stuff and paranoia—it's horrible." She dabbed the pencil on my other eyelid, the point of her tongue peeking from the corner of her mouth as she made a final stroke. "He loved us, though."

"People who love each other don't hurt each other. Or abandon you."

She lowered the pencil, the corner of her mouth pulling into smile. "Are you kidding?"

"Not like that, they don't," I said. "I don't think that's love."

"Aww." She kissed my cheek. "Don't get all worked up. Maybe it's not. Or maybe it's just love that sucks." She reached out and pressed her palms on my bare shoulders. "Whatevs. You can look now."

I turned back toward the mirror and hardly recognized myself. My eyes gleamed, blue irises outlined in black. My hair was wild and violet. Lindsay kissed me between the shoulder blades and then looped her arms under my own. Standing behind me, she rested her fingertips on my collarbones, her lean forearms crisscrossed with scars, and put her chin on my shoulder. Her eyes shone beside mine in the mirror, her cotton T-shirt pressing against my back, her breath warm on my ear.

"Look," she said. "There we are. Aren't we beautiful together?"

It was how I'd always want to remember us: looking at ourselves, looking at each other, all made up with no one else around to see.

She said, "It looks good. Admit it."

"Yeah," I said, "but it's not really me."

Weeks became months. Lindsay and I passed our notes, hung out at the waffle place, and chatted online. We fooled around in her Taurus and caught movies on weekends. For Valentine's Day, she bought me a studded bracelet (not really my style), I got her a skull-and-crossbones pendant. For our two month, she got me an illustrated book of William Blake poems. I'd gotten her a black tank top with tiny bats printed all over it.

I still rode to school with Erik in the morning, but we hadn't been hanging out nearly as much after school. Most of my free time was taken up with homework and my girlfriend. Most of his, it seemed, was spent hanging out at the Farm. He and Pink Dick were putting a band together and, from what I heard, out of their skulls all the time. It bothered me a bit. I didn't think much good came from being out there. I didn't want Dick to replace me, either. For the most part, though, I felt great about things. The winter ice thawed, tulips poked through the ground, and for the moment, I'd forgotten about the Y2K bug, my college applications, and other world-ending scenarios. Much to my own surprise, I was thinking about prom.

I'd always said I'd never consider going. But now, as the year wound down, I kind of wanted to. I mainly wanted a picture of Lindsay and I dressed up like European aristocrats, and maybe for us to be able to spend a whole night together. It was at the end of May, almost two months away, but I was excited. Sitting in English class, I decided I'd ask her after school.

Our English class was reading *Romeo and Juliet* aloud that day. We'd read it before, as freshmen, but some touring company was coming to school to perform it, so we were all reading it again. Each role for the day was assigned to someone. When we got to the part where Tybalt stabs Mercutio, Erik was reading the part of Mercutio.

Romeo asks Mercutio about his wound. And Mercutio says, "No, 'tis not so deep as a well, nor so wide as a church-door; but 'tis enough, 'twill serve: ask for me to-morrow, and you shall find me a grave man."

Erik read that part, and he laughed.

The class laughed, too. I don't know if they really got it, or if they were just responding to him the way stupid people do to laugh tracks on TV.

Anyway, this is the thing. He kept laughing. He tried to keep it in, but he kept bursting out. I mean, it was *insane*. He could hardly breathe. Mr. Hartigan had to make some else read Mercutio because Erik couldn't say his lines anymore. He was purple-faced, shaking, trying to cage in his laughter.

Everybody started to get kind of freaked out because Erik kept breaking into fits of giggles in the back. Mr. Hartigan warned him that he was being disruptive.

"What's your deal?" I whispered harshly to Erik. "It's not that funny."

"A *grave* man," he responded, and then exploded into another fit of hysterics.

Eventually, Mr. Hartigan decided Erik was on drugs and sent him to the nurse. I didn't think that was the problem. Maybe he was just unprepared for the Bard's rapier-sharp wit. Maybe acting out his own death made something come unhinged in his head. Maybe he was just trying to make Mr. Hartigan have another coronary. I had no idea. After an hour in the nurse's office, he was sent back to class. For the rest of the day, people were saying he was on acid.

After school, I found Lindsay sitting on the curb near Smoker's Corner. Since she lived so close to the grounds, she usually walked home with Amanda. The two of them sat on the curb, smoking, Lindsay's pink knees peeking through holes in her stockings. A robin hopped around in the muddy grass behind them. Pink Dick and some other kids stood nearby, taking turns trying to throw a knife into a tree. I sat down next to her, and she put her head on my shoulder.

"Is this year ever going to end?" she asked.

"No," I said. "I think we're dead. Maybe this is Hell."

"Hell would have cooler people."

"So, I was thinking," I said, "you want to go to prom with me?"

Her laughter was a slap in the face.

"Omigod, I'm sorry," she said. "You're serious. You actually want to go?"

"Kinda," I said. "I don't know. You don't have to be mean about it."

"Sorry, baby." She kissed me on the cheek. "I'll do anything for love, but I won't to that. We can do something else. Anything. You name it."

"Fine."

I looked away, my face hot. Dick threw the knife, and it stuck point-first into the tree with a dull *thunk*. A few kids clapped. Erik's car rolled up, the double-bass drumming of some Scandinavian death metal blazing on the stereo. He buzzed down the window and asked if I needed a ride.

"See you later," I said to Lindsay.

She opened her arms to hug me, but I just pulled on my backpack and got in the car without even looking back.

Erik and I headed down to Arthur's Pond. This was the first day since winter that it seemed warm enough to go there. It was in the woods that backed up onto my subdivision, in a small clearing at the bottom of a ravine. Tall reeds and cattails swayed in its shallows, and an outcropping of glacial boulders formed a short peninsula into it. The jade-green water stood still as glass. In order to get to the pond, we followed a narrow deer trail through otherwise impassible brambles and undergrowth. It was our place to reflect, philosophize, and hide. We called it Arthur's Pond because it looked like something from a legend—like a magic sword might rest somewhere in its emerald depths.

Even though the trees were bare, traces of green rose in the cool spring afternoon. Sunlight dappled the mossy rocks and reflected on the pond. Erik seemed troubled, more so than usual, and not just because of the laughing jag during English class.

A dark aura seemed to whirl around him. He sat on a stump, leafing through his Doomsday Book, pausing to sip from a military canteen or drag on his cigarette. I sat with my backpack at my feet, tossing acorns into the water and watching the ripples spread out in perfect concentric circles.

"What's in that thing, anyway?" I asked.

"You'll find out when the world ends," he said. "Be patient."

"Not the book." I tossed another acorn into the water. "I meant the flask."

"Oh." He gave a sheepish smile. "A mix of everything in the liquor cabinet. Take a little from every bottle, and it doesn't look like much is gone."

"Yuck," I said. "Why the hell would you do that to yourself?"

"I got problems," he said.

"Yeah," I said. "What was with you in Hartigan's class today?"

"Oh, that? Mercutio's line was funny, that's all." He took a swig. "I wasn't expecting it."

"We read it in ninth grade."

"I wasn't expecting it to get to me. Like, how sad it was that he got killed over something so dumb."

"You thought that was funny?"

"Not really. I guess I was scared that if I didn't keep laughing, I might, you know..." He gave an embarrassed grin. "I got problems."

"Yeah," I said. "Me too. I asked Lindsay to prom."

He laughed. "That's your problem?"

"She said no," I said. "After we've been going out for like three months. Almost three. I mean, what the hell? I know she's too cool for everything, but come on."

"She probably just doesn't feel comfortable," he said. "With prom. Maybe it's just not her thing."

"Prom isn't *anybody's* thing," I said. "But still."

"She's really into you, dude. I don't know what you're worried about."

"How do you know she's so into me?"

"It's obvious." He sipped from the canteen and then made a pucker face. "That, and she talks about you all the time. Here, will you put this in your bag till we get back?"

He stood and handed me his book. I slid it into my backpack.

"Wait," I said. "She talks about me all the time when?"

Erik walked to a low-hanging limb and hoisted himself onto it. "When we talk," he said. "Me and her."

"I didn't know you guys talked," I said.

"There's lots of shit you don't know."

My jaw tightened. He climbed to a higher branch.

"Like what?"

He was quiet for a moment.

"My mom moved out of the house," he said, his legs dangling in the air. His cockiness was gone, and his voice was hushed, softer, more like a child's. "I think they're splitting up. I don't know what's going on, and neither of them will talk to me about it."

I had a flash of Mr. Grundler embracing the black-haired woman in the hot tub on the day after Christmas, and sadness passed over me like the shadow of a cloud. There was lots of shit Erik didn't know, either.

"How long has she been gone?"

"Since the beginning of March," he said. "She's with my aunt right now."

Even though so many kids I'd known growing up had divorced parents, it was something I never worried about happening to my family. The thought of my mom packing a suitcase and leaving us, or my dad solemnly loading up a U-Haul and driving away would have hit me like napalm dropped on our home from the sky.

"I'm sorry," I said. "Why didn't you tell me?"

He lifted his open hands and swayed on the branch where he sat. I worried he might fall.

"What difference would it make?" he said. "Everybody gets divorced, pretty much. It's not a big deal." He sighed. "But there's only so much I can't give shit about, you know?"

I got home in time for dinner. After we ate, I saw all of the crazy crap on the evening news and decided that I was being too hard on Lindsay. She probably never planned on anyone taking her seriously enough to go to prom with her. I knew everyone probably thought I was stupid for loving her. She was just a self-involved suicide drama queen with more issues than National Geographic, a trashy-looking girl with sub-par spelling, a head full of vampire novels, and some pretty bad taste in music. But she was beautiful to me. Not just because of how she looked and smiled, hurt and hated, but because she was sincere and real and sad. I wanted to hold her and need her, and I had every expectation that it wouldn't work out like I wanted it to, but that would be okay as long as I got to have her for awhile. She was what I thought life would probably be like for me. I didn't expect anyone to understand it.

I spread out on the floor of my bedroom to do my homework.

When I zipped open my backpack to get out my notes, I realized Erik had left the Doomsday Book with me. The cold dead skin of its leather cover exhilarated and repelled me as I pulled it out of the bag and opened it.

It was all plain, unlined paper, filled with Erik's jagged handwriting and sketches. Quotes from Goebbels and Julius Caesar. Lyrics from heavy metal songs. His poems. Erik's sketches, the standard fare for him: skulls, demons, killer robots, armored tanks, wolves, stuff like that. But strangest of all were the maps and photos.

He had sketched overhead maps of several local spots, with scale notations. A few other photos of places on Main Street were glued in place, too, places like the gazebo, the barbershop, and the cemetery. But the most space was devoted to Birch Hills High. He'd laid out the corridors and rooms in painstaking detail, with annotations like "partial cover," "full cover," and "optimum casualty zone." One page was covered with huge letters reading, "With a Bang."

I closed the book, feeling sorry that I'd looked into Erik's bloodthirsty power fantasy. Sorry for him, too. *It was only a joke*, I told myself. *It had to be. Nothing more.* I decided to take the book back to him right then. If my mom found it, she would totally freak out.

Mr. Grundler answered the door at Erik's place, dressed in a tracksuit and holding a glass of scotch. I had a flash of the woman going down on him in the hot tub, and I squirmed.

"Erik left one of his books with me," I said. "I thought he'd want it back."

"Sure, sure," Mr. Grunder said. He screamed Erik's name up the stairs then walked back to the couch.

Erik came down the steps, struggling to close up the last few buttons of his black work shirt. He'd put it on in a hurry; the buttons weren't lined up right.

"What's up?" he said, smiling, then hugged me with one arm. He usually didn't touch anyone.

"You left this in my bag," I said, holding the Doomsday Book out to him.

"Wow. Thanks for bringing it by," he said, grabbing it out from my hands. "Some master planner I am, eh? Well, I'm wiped, dude. I guess I'll see you tomorrow."

"Um, okay."

Then I saw it, hanging from the banner on the stairs. It was a military surplus bag, stenciled with the words KILL YOURSELF, NOW. A tiny pair of combat boots sat on the floor beneath it. Lindsay was there, up in his room. My stomach boiled, and my head felt like a volcano erupting.

"I—" I looked around, unsure for a moment were I was, the glass ceiling of the foyer showing only night. "I have to go home."

10

The next morning, I rode to school with Erik but hardly said a word. Lindsay had called three times since the night before, but I didn't pick up. I wanted to talk to her in person. Erik seemed cool as ever. He smoked a cigarette in the blue morning as he drove, flipping through the radio stations. We never spoke much on the morning drive, so my silence didn't seem unusual. His locker was in east wing, mine in west, so we parted ways naturally enough, too.

I passed her in the hall on my way to homeroom. She was wearing a Misfits shirt with the sleeves cut off, leaning against her locker by Amanda and Li. When she brightly called after me, I hurried onward through the crowd.

A few hours later, in the art room before class started, she sat down next to me and put her head on my shoulder. I shrugged it off.

"Hey." She scrunched her nose for a moment. "I saw you this morning in west wing. I yelled at you."

"I know. You were talking to Li."

"Yeah. I tried calling you last night, too."

"What were you and Li talking about?"

"Huh? I don't remember. You know, we were just hanging out."

"Do you like him?"

"Chigger?" She laughed. "I mean, he's okay."

She squeezed my knee, and I tensed.

"Are you still mad about me not wanting to go to prom? If it's really that important—"

I pulled her hand off of my leg and said, "It's more than that."

Her face blanked, and she said, "What's more than that?"

Before I could answer, Pink Dick walked up. He wore the black-finished cat's head from the first art project around his neck like a medallion.

"Jocks pissed on my gym clothes, and the teacher still gave me a no-dress. Like I should wear 'em anyways. One more no-dress and I don't pass. I hate this fuckin' place." He looked from me to Lindsay and asked, "What happened to you guys?"

"We'll talk later," I told her.

Li skipped class, and Dick sensed the tension, so he ignored us. For the rest of the period, I tried to stay focused on my "fantasy handscape" drawing assignment. We were supposed use our own hands as models in some surreal or fantasy composition. Mine showed a knight fighting a dragon made out of hands; two with fingers spread wide formed the wings, a third in the center made the body, its curved index finger rained fire down at St. George.

Lindsay had drawn her own forearm and hand as a tree. Crows roosted on her fingers, and her scars became splits in the bark, torn open by still smaller hands trying to claw their way out from inside.

Lindsay and I went to our hidey hall after the bell rang, and I threw up the question.

"Where were you last night?"

"What?" She set down her bag. "I was at home, where else?"

"Okay. How about around seven-thirty? Last night."

"I was at home. Jesus, am I under arrest?"

"I'm serious."

"So, I have to tell you my every move?" She scowled. "I've been trying to call you since yesterday, and you haven't picked up. You don't see me hassling you about it."

"Because you know I wouldn't cheat on you."

"Oh, but I would on you?"

I was quiet a moment before asking, "Were you with Erik?"

"What do you mean, 'with?'"

"You know exactly what I mean."

"You're asking if I fucked him?"

"No," I snapped. "Why, did you?"

She flinched and then said, "You're asking me if I screwed your best friend? You really think I'd do that?"

"Well, I know some of the things you've done in the past, Linds."

It was a stupid thing to say. What I was trying to tell her was how scared I was. That I thought what we had was special and beautiful, and I worried that she didn't know that or didn't feel that way, too. Both she and Erik had an intensity I thought I lacked. I feared they'd become drawn to one another—and away from me. I didn't know what was happening anymore. The universe, like Erik had said, didn't even know what time it was. She picked up her bag and threw it over her shoulder.

"You know, a lot of people think a lot of things about me. But I never thought you were one of them. I didn't do anything wrong. What is your problem?"

"You're the one with problems," I said. "You don't see me cutting myself, sneaking around, and then getting all self-righteous about it."

"I can't believe I thought you were different. I was actually going to go to the prom with you."

"Lindsay, I was over there last night and—"

"He's your friend. But you think he's a user, and that I'm just some stupid whore."

"Hey, I never said—"

"Of course not. Nice guys never say it, but I know what you think. Let's just forget about this. We're done."

She hurried away, swallowed up by the crowd. We had broken up. Just like that. I walked down the chokingly crowded hall. My chest was tight and something felt wrong with my right hand. I realized it was the first time since winter break that I'd gone to sixth hour without Lindsay's girl-folded note from her clutched in my sweaty palm. There was nothing to look forward to.

Erik and I sat at Pizza Cove after school, sharing a double cheese with ham and pineapple. Sun poured into the restaurant's dining area, the red plastic tabletops and yellow tiled floor seemed oppressively colorful in its light.

"Man," Erik said, his mouth full of food. "I'm never getting married. It never works."

"My parents are still together."

He grunted and swallowed. "You're being too literal about things. I mean, I could never settle on one person forever. I don't think most people can. It's not natural."

I had a flash of Lindsay's nakedness curled against me and thought of her taste: smoke and soda pop.

"Is that why you nail whatever beer-drunk skank happens to fall on her back for you?" I asked.

He blinked and then smiled.

"Some of them are sober when they fall on their backs for me. Like your mom, for example."

"Clever." If he wanted to needle me about my folks, I certainly could poke back. "You ever consider that maybe an attitude like that is why *your* parents are splitting up?"

"Probably," he said. "He fucked around on her enough. I mean, if I knew about it, I'm sure she figured it out eventually."

"Wait." I tread carefully, careful for a trap. "You think he was having an affair?"

"No. Not 'an.' Several."

"How'd you find out?"

"I'd rather not talk about it. Thanks." He looked out the front window, out onto the main road, as if gazing over the sea. "Let's just say my car was purchased with silence. You think my dad bought me that NSX just for being such a great kid?"

"Are you serious?"

"Take it how you can get it," he said and then added, "I'm never getting married. That's all."

We were both quiet for a moment. Erik took a sip of his Coke. I blew my nose in a napkin. He looked up at me and asked if I'd ever seen *Shock Waves*. It was a monster movie about undead, black-goggled Nazis who lived underwater. I hadn't seen it.

The conversation's gravity evaporated as Erik and I prattled on about how lame most vampire movies were when compared to zombie movies, which segued into whether or not Frankenstein's monster was a zombie, and then to our wondering if the risen Christ counted as "undead." This topic meandered into the Catholic rite of Communion, where wine was transmuted into the Blood of Our Savior to be consumed by believers.

"Therefore," Erik said, "all Christians worship a Jewish zombie, but Catholics are *vampires* who worship a Jewish zombie. It's a small distinction, but an important one."

He pulled the Doomsday Book out of his bag and wrote a note inside of it. I picked at my slice.

"Well?" He seemed annoyed by my silence. "You're Catholic. I need some input on this."

"We only go on High Holy days. But I can tell you that Frankenstein's monster isn't a zombie." I said. "Zombies don't have complex feelings. They're just dead and walking around."

He considered this.

"I guess you're right. Frankenstein's monster wants revenge against its maker. Zombies just want to make more zombies."

"Not even that," I said. "They just want to eat brains. Any other result is incidental."

A giant, brown Jeep rolled through the lot, blasting some radio-friendly prep punk. Dustin Lake, one of the guys who'd beaten up Erik at Taco Bell last year, drove. Another couple of dudes from the meathead jock-patrol lurked in the passenger seat and in back.

"Speaking of mindless hordes," he said. "We should get out of here."

Erik shoved his book back in his bag, dumped what was left of the pizza into the trash, and we headed out.

We found his car had been egged in the lot. More like bombarded, actually. Bits of shell flecked the black paint, and the yolks swirled in translucent slime dripping down its windshield and hood. Erik's chest rose and fell as he took a single heaving breath. He placed his hands on his hips. The Jeep sped away onto the main road, its windows down so we could hear their catcalls.

"You know the best way to take down a zombie?" Erik asked, fishing keys from his pocket.

The egg-gunk oozed and dripped, making the car look like a sleek black monster covered with afterbirth. I felt as if I were sinking down into the asphalt. Everyone knew the best way to take down a zombie was to shoot it in the head.

We drove through an automated car wash on the way back to the neighborhood. Sprayers blanketed the windshield with opalescent cleansers as the conveyor pulled us through.

"This reminds me of therapy." Erik leaned back in his seat. "You come out polished up, but still a mess inside."

He'd hugged me the night he'd come down from being with my girlfriend, I thought. They'd been doing it the whole time, and I was too dumb to see it. That's why he'd said, "I'm not mad" when I first hooked up with her. And Pink Dick sneered about Linds and me, saying "She's probably scamming," and then Erik had nudged him to shut up. On the way back from the truck stop, she'd said of Erik, "Everybody has to have some secrets." Everyone had known but me. That was so messed up. Bile washed up in the back of my throat.

"Poor you," I said.

"What?"

"It must be tough to have rich parents, an awesome car, and a ton of drugs and sex. And a therapist to listen to all your problems."

When the rotating brushes began to vibrate the car, it seemed as if the tunnel of machinery moved around us while we stood still, closing us in and shaking us apart.

"Hey," he looked over at me, his head tilted to the side. "Why are you being such a dick? You don't think I have enough shit to deal with?"

"God knows, you're the only one who has shit to deal with, right?"

The huge blowers roared their hurricane as the conveyors dragged us into the light.

"What's going on, Josh?"

"What do you care?" I turned to look out the window as we

pulled out of the car wash. "Just drop me off somewhere, okay? Please?"

We drove into Whispering Meadows subdivision and passed my house.

"Where are we going?"

"Arthur's Pond."

"Why?"

"So we can straighten some things out. If you can't stand it when we get there, you can leave."

"Fine."

We parked in the cul-de-sac and made our way down the slope and through the woods. The path was thick with leaves and brambles by then. I followed a few steps behind Erik, watching him pass through jagged nets of shadow. Oily feelings broiled in my head, telling me to trip him, to push him, to grab him by the shoulders and scream in his face. I stopped walking and said, "I broke up with Lindsay."

"What?" He turned to face me. "Because she didn't want to go to prom?"

"She wasn't who I thought she was." Then I added, "I don't know if you are, either."

"Alright, whatever. What are you saying?"

My breath came faster, sharper, and my heart pounded.

"Did you—" The f-word lodged in my throat. I swallowed and tried it differently, the question emerging as a strained rasp, the childishness of its phrasing only upsetting me more. "Did you do it with her?"

"What?" He raised both his hands. "Dude, what kind of question is that?"

"Did you?"

"Do it? You mean, like, did we ever fuck?"

"So you did."

"I didn't say that. I just wanted to know if you meant—"

"If 'ever' makes a difference, then you did."

"Look." He lowered his chin. "What she did before you two were together—"

"What about after? Huh? The night I came back to deliver your book, I saw her purse on the railing. And her boots. She was in your room, and you had your shirt off."

"Whoa. Hold on. We're just friends—"

"Friends like your drunk dad and the trailer trash woman he goes hot-tubbing with? You're just like him. You all do it to yourselves, then you whine—"

My words broke into a grunt when he buried his fist into my solar plexus. Stumbling, I swung lamely at him and missed. I fell into a tangle of undergrowth, losing my glasses.

"You don't know shit," he shouted.

I started to get up, but he kicked me in the ribs. A guttural retch burbled from my throat when I rolled onto the path. Dry leaves stuck to my face, and dirt seeped into my mouth.

"You don't know me, or my family, and you sure as fuck don't know Lindsay."

I huddled on the ground, unable to get my breath back.

"You don't know." He shambled a few steps, then stooped over to pick up a grapefruit-sized rock.

"What are you doing?" I coughed, gasping, "Jesus Christ."

He looked at the rock as if it had mysteriously appeared in his hand. It fell from his grip and thumped into the dirt. Erik sat down on a log and put his hands over his face. The scar across his knuckles puckered when he pressed his forehead.

"You were going to hit me with that?" I dragged myself onto my side, trying not to whimper from the pain blossoming in my torso. "You psycho."

"Lindsay wasn't who you thought?" he snapped, his face scarlet and his mouth twisted. "She's Lindsay. And I'm me. And if you don't know who we are, then that's your problem."

"I loved her." I said.

"You *loved* her? You don't even know what that means. You loved her. Give me a break."

"What were you doing with her?"

"Now you want to talk about it? No way. I'm gone." He stormed back down the path, mumbling, "Someday, you'll see how psycho I really can be."

I stood up, unsteady, yelling after him, "You do it to yourselves."

I brushed the burrs from my coat, ignoring the wetness streaming down my face, beaten and alone in the woods, without my glasses. Birds sang, wind sighed, and the sun sank in the sky as if nothing had happened at all.

11

I waited for the school bus with three middle-school kids: two half-asleep guys who played Gameboys, and a puffy-coated girl who listened to headphones. They lived in my neighborhood, but I didn't know whose kids they were; I hadn't ridden the bus in a couple years. We stood at the entrance to Whispering Meadows in a shifting semicircle across from the traffic island. Erik's car rumbled up to the shoulder, and its tinted window buzzed open.

"I stopped by your house," he said.

I ignored him. My ribs still ached from his kick the day before. Across the street, a golden retriever bounced up and down in a house's picture window, its barks muted by the glass. The girl softly hummed the melody of some pop-punk song. He revved the engine.

"Come on, dude, get in."

"No."

"You're a senior. You can't ride the cheese to school."

"Why? So you can bash my head in with a rock after you screw my girlfriend?"

The Gameboy kids smirked but didn't look up from their screens.

"Look, neither of those things happened." Before I could respond, he added, "I'll explain on the way. Just think of it as using me for my car for right now."

I shuffled my feet and sighed.

"I'm really sorry I lost my temper," he said, adding, "I'll buy you breakfast," in a sing-song voice. "Please?"

I saw the bus in the distance, the red lights over its windshield alternating left-right-left, and despaired at the thought of riding alone with all the underclassmen and middle schoolers. I looked back to Erik, who desperately motioned for me to climb in, as though the bus might take me away to some inescapably desolate place. I mumbled something and gave in. The door slammed behind me. I wouldn't look at him.

After a few minutes of driving, he said, "I didn't do anything with Lindsay. I swear to God."

"You don't believe in God."

"What do you want me to swear to, then?"

I didn't answer.

"What makes you think we did it?"

"My ribs still hurt," I said, ignoring the question. "And you were going to hit me with that rock."

"Dude, you went really low with that shit about my dad. You've never been like that to me before."

"Like what?"

"I don't know," he said. "Mean. It freaked me out a bit."

"Yeah, well you definitely out-freaked me by beating me up."

"I'm sorry." His shoulders slumped in the driver's seat. "When I'm hurt, I don't think. I just lash out."

"Yeah, that'll work out well for you, I'm sure. What were you doing with Lindsay?"

"Trying to convince her to go to prom with you."

"In your bedroom? With your shirt off?"

He rolled his eyes so hard his head tilted back. "I spilled bong water all over the other one. I'd just changed it."

"Bull. It was the same black work shirt you had on earlier."

"No, it wasn't. I have three of them." We stopped short at the corner of Harker and Grand River, my seatbelt pulling tight. A UPS truck's back end blotted out the windshield. He pointed at me, saying, "You know that."

"You have three black work shirts? Why would I know that? I inventory your clothes?"

"Well, there was nothing going on."

"I don't believe you."

The light changed, and we made a right onto Grand River. Erik floored it to pass the delivery truck, and then cut sharply back into the lane. The truck honked. He flipped it off over his shoulder.

"You don't know what happened," he said. "Lindsay and I do. I'm telling you. I have other girls to fool around with. I wouldn't do it with yours. You can believe me, and everything'll be cool, or you can think I suck and am lying, and we won't be friends anymore, and everything's ruined. Up to you."

"It's not a decision like that. You don't just decide what reality is. You figure it out."

"Oh, really? Then what is it?"

"I don't know," I said. "Things are weird lately."

"Do you want to skip homeroom and get some pancakes?"

I nodded. I'd refused my mom's oatmeal on the way out, and I was hungry. I wasn't any surer of anything after a blueberry short-stack than I was before. Erik and I didn't talk about much. We just ate together.

I missed homeroom for the first time that year, checked in with the office, and went to first hour. By the time art class rolled around, I still had no idea what to do about the Lindsay situation, or if I should believe Erik, or what. My stomach boiled.

As it turned out, Lindsay didn't show up to art class. Pink Dick and Li hadn't seen her, either. Her empty stool sat there like a missing panel in a mural. After class, Amanda shoved her way across the hall and rolled up on me at my locker. I braced myself.

"Lindsay told me to give you this," she said.

I flinched, expecting her to slap me, but instead she thrust out a perfectly square girl-folded note. Amanda glared at me when I took it, her blue eyes cutting me from beneath silver-painted lids. A pink thong met my eyes like an accusation as she stomped away.

I slouched my way into the library for study hall. Erik was already at our usual table, sandwiched between a rectangular pillar and the biography section. Everything smelled like pencil shavings and mildew. A quiet and orderly place unlike anywhere else in school, I usually felt safe there, but that day I didn't. Erik looked up and gave me a nod. Messy stacks of books on military history, commando training, and SWAT tactics laid on the tabletop. I dropped my bag to the floor and slid into a seat across from him.

"If the Grim Reaper had a cock," he said, "it would look like the AK-47."

"Whatever." I leaned back and dug the note out my pocket. It tucked into itself with that secret origami all girls seem to master by the end of second grade. I flattened it out on the table and read it.

Dear Josh—

I wish I'd told you I was with Erik when you asked. But I was worried that you'd think I was up to something. But you already thought I was anyway. I know I made it look worse but I had no idea you thought I was such a crappy person. We both think bad things about each other now. We don't trust each other. You're never going to believe me like before + I'm always going to think you look down on me. Maybe we can be friends?

Luvz,

Lindsay

I tore the note into pieces before noisily pulling a Rimbaud paperback from my pack. Erik didn't look up. He hunched over the Doomsday Book, his pencil scritch-scratching in a frenzy as he drew. A photo book of the Vietnam War lay open on the tabletop in front him. Behind him, a wall of water-stained windows on the library's east side provided a view of two scrubby trees, an expanse of sod, and the visitor parking lot—not very majestic, but better than the white cinderblock you saw everywhere else. A few seconds after flipping one of the book's big, glossy pages, Erik went, "Whoa, Josh. You should take a look at this."

I glanced over the top of my book. He tapped his pencil's eraser rapidly on one of the photos. Whatever atrocity he'd discovered, napalm-crisped corpses or a bullet-riddled water buffalo, I didn't want to see it. I had enough bad stuff running around in my head as it was.

"I'm reading right now. It's *poetry*. Get it? I need to concentrate."

"It's not too gross or anything, but dude," he said, "I think it's your dad."

"Look, I've had about enough insane crap lately." I sat up straight, put down my book, and glared at him. "You're lucky I'm even sitting with you."

Erik spun the volume around to face me and then pushed it to the center, as if raising me an encyclopedia-sized pile of poker chips. His index finger stabbed like a crow's beak against a grainy black-and-white photo on the page.

"Check it out," he said triumphantly.

It was the soldier's smile I noticed first, a recognition that pulled my heart into my stomach. It was Dad's smile, one that turned down at the corners across his long face. A cigarette, or maybe a joint, dangled between his lips. The shirtless man in the picture was tall and lanky, like me, but thicker and more imposing. A set of dog tags hung between a pair of tiny bull's-eye nipples. I'd dyed my hair purple and wore glasses, but traces of his face reflected in my own: the high forehead, the pointed chin. He looked a little bit older than me. A helmet, tipped to one side, sat jauntily atop his head. One hand flashed the peace sign, the other propped the stock of an M-16 against his hip.

He stood with one boot placed on the back of a dead man. The corpse's hands and feet were a shade lighter than the muddy earth on which it laid—facedown, anonymous, and crumpled. A black halo of blood pooled around its head. The background was out-of-focus, a swath of jungle green turned news photo gray. The soldier's image, formed from the captured light of 1969, stared up from the page at his future son.

"Jesus," I whispered.

"Unidentified U.S. soldier poses with enemy casualty, 1969," Erik said, quoting the caption. "It's really him, isn't it?"

His leather jacket creaked as he shifted in his chair. I stared down at the picture like I was peeking over a canyon's edge, and I was sickened by its depth.

Erik cleared his throat before saying, "It's good to see he kept his sense of irony over there, at least." He pointed his pencil at the hand holding up the peace sign.

I looked up and said, "I guess."

"I'm not making fun of it, believe me. My dad got a deferment and a record contract."

Just then the bell rang, and I jerked as if it had sneaked up and grabbed me. I peeked around the pillar, checking if the librarian was watching, and then ripped the page from the book in a single pull. Guilt stabbed my chest; I never imagined I'd vandalize a library book. I folded the sheet into quarters, stood up, and shoved it in my back pocket.

Erik closed the book, put it back on the shelf, and then we both headed to class.

The hallways were jammed, as always. I cursed the town for voting down the proposal to expand, leaving the place more overcrowded than a Detroit jail. Students formed two lanes of foot traffic out of necessity. Once you got into one, the weight of the crowd became a river, pushing you along. Erik made cow noises, as always, and several guys mooed back as they shoved past. I felt the dark heft of the Vietnam photo crumpled in my pocket as the human current pulled me along.

The roaring noise and suffocating weight of the crowd made my head heavy and my breathing short. The edges of my vision became gray and fuzzy as I plodded along with the hordes. I somehow made it to fifth hour. My head cleared up a bit in Mr. Wolcott's biology class. I couldn't pay attention to mitosis or meiosis or anything, but I felt a bit less out-of-whack. I'd always figured there was stuff in Dad's past I didn't want to know about. I thought it was all the regular stuff people's parents did in the sixties that you don't want to hear, though. Like smoking pot, free love, and being naked in public. The sort of thing Mr. Grundler probably had done, and it seemed had never stopped doing.

But my dad had killed people.

"We each began as a single cell," Mr. Wolcott announced. He pointed at what looked like a fried egg he'd drawn on the dry-erase board. "Now, each person in here is made of a *trillion* cells. Can you imagine? A stack of a trillion sheets of paper could reach to the moon and back—*twenty-five times!*"

He waited for a reaction. Shannon Szwerski cracked her gum. Somebody coughed. I fidgeted in my tiny desk, unsure how to arrange my legs. Wolcott sighed and continued his lesson.

I remembered my dad shooting the squirrel from Paul's bedroom window. How he'd looked as if he didn't recognize me after he pulled the trigger.

"…it's a rough process, and it's not perfect." Mr. Wolcott smiled like an excited game show host. "The cells' organelles are destroyed and then remade in just a few hours. If the replication messes up, things like cancer and other genetic diseases can occur. But usually, replication is identical…"

His voice melted into an undecipherable drone. My face tingled, and my brain somersaulted inside my skull. The room stretched out in all directions, pulled by a funhouse mirror, so I stared at the floor. The white glare of light against linoleum hurt my eyes. I put my head down, cradled it in my arms, and sank into the dark warmth.

I yelped awake when a hand grasped my shoulder. Florescent lights buzzed over the emptied classroom, cycling with the dull roar of mobs passing in the hallway beyond. A couple giggling girls looked over their shoulders as they went out the door.

Mr. Wolcott stood over my desk with a look of concern across his stubbly face. His tie's knot was crooked.

"Josh, class is over. You fell asleep." He leaned forward and looked at me. "Are you okay?"

I nodded. A puddle of drool glistened on my desktop, so I wiped it up with my shirtsleeve.

"Are you sick?" Mr. Wolcott asked. "Do you need to see the nurse?"

"I'm not on drugs," I snapped.

"I know you're not," he said, smiling, "but you *never* sleep in class."

"I'm stressed out." I unfolded my legs from beneath the desktop and stood up. "Sometimes I just get really tired. It happens. I'm sorry."

"Trouble at home? Anything you want to talk about?"

"No. Thanks. It won't happen again."

Mr. Wolcott patted me on the shoulder, stiff-armed and awkward.

"I'm late for my next class," I said. "See you tomorrow."

I slid my hand into my back pocket as I walked out the door, feeling the glossy page crinkle under my fingers. I wanted to look at what repelled me. I'd had enough of backing down.

12

The rest of the day passed in a haze. Erik and I stopped by the Gas-Go on the way home from school and then hung out in its parking lot. I sat on the curb, drinking a Strawberry Freezie. He leaned on his sleek, black car and chain smoked. With an undertaker's seriousness, he explained that you could tell what color pubic hair a girl had by her eyebrows.

"As above, so below," he said. Erik flicked the butt of his cigarette at a nearby sparrow, which retreated in fluttering terror. "That's an occult truth. Wizards used to talk about this shit."

Considering my suspicions about him and Lindsay, it didn't make for good conversation. I sighed as a huge, brown jeep drove through the lot, full of meatheads. One of them yelled "faggots" at us as it passed.

The car they'd egged last week was Erik's, not mine. And I'd been called a faggot more times than I could count in Birch Hills. Obviously, if it really bothered me, I wouldn't have let Lindsay dye my hair purple. But something different happened inside of me this time.

I stood up and ran after the jeep. With all my strength, I hurled my Freezie, screaming "Fuck you!" at the top of my lungs. It hit the Jeep with a splat, covering its back window with a bright pink explosion of gooey slime. The brake lights burned red, like three glowing eyes shining back at me, as it halted.

"Whoa," Erik said. "Good throw."

The doors swung open and three guys got out, the biggest of whom was Dustin Lake, the driver, a slab of beef and hair gel stuffed into a letterman jacket. He ran to the back of his jeep, and when he saw the Freezie splatter, pointed his finger at me and yelled, "You're dead, homo!"

"Dammit," Erik said. "Here we go again. Let me handle this."

But I was already running—not away, for once, but at Dustin. I barreled toward him, my legs pumping, rage flowing through every vein. He looked at me like he couldn't quite make sense of what was happening. I plowed into him with my shoulder and slammed him against the back of the jeep, knocking the wind from him. I couldn't let up. Before he could un-hunch himself, I started furiously punching—and landing, too, sick fleshy thuds against my knuckles. He held me around the waist, ducking down. Pain exploded in my right hand as my fist cracked against his skull.

"Kill you!" I screamed. "Fucking kill you!"

A bright flash of light spun me around. I'd been struck dead in the nose. Pain shot through my twisting ankle, and the pavement hit me next, biting into my cheekbone. Someone kicked me in the stomach before I could get up. I grunted and folded in half, the air wooshing out of me. I'd forgotten about the other two guys. I heard Dustin spit, it might've been on me, and then he said, "Hold this pussy up so I can hit him."

"Get away from him!" Erik screamed.

I struggled to sit up. Erik stood in front of the guys, his stance wide. There was a small spray can in his right hand, and he pointed it at them like a six-shooter.

"I'll put Mace in your eyes. I'll burn 'em right out."

"Oh, you gonna use Mace on me, like some bitch?" Dustin said, thumping his chest. "You just proved you're a faggot."

"That's right," Erik replied, "and once I have you blind and retching on the ground, I'm going to pull down your pants and pump your sweet ass full of my cum."

"What?" Dustin said.

"That's right. I'm going to blind you and tear up your shitter. I might go to prison, but everyone will know what I did to you. Try me."

"You're fuckin' sick," gasped one of Dustin's lackeys, a doughy guy in a brown leather jacket.

"Tell me about it," Erik said, raising an eyebrow. "Get the fuck out of here before you find out how sick I really am."

"Let's go," Dustin said, punching one of his buddies on the arm. "We don't want to get these guys' AIDS blood on us."

As the Jeep pulled away, I started laughing. Erik helped me up and slapped me on the back. My whole body ached, and my nose bled down my chin.

"Nice work," he said. "Kamikaze attack. Very honorable."

"I didn't know you carried Mace," I said.

He shoved me. "I don't. I'm not a bitch."

He handed me the little canister as I limped to the car beside him. It was a can of Ozium air freshener.

"For when I blaze-up in the car," he explained. "Deception is the most versatile of weapons. By the way, do know what you look like right now?"

"Like a guy who just got his ass beat in a parking lot."

"Exactly. Call your mom and tell her you won't be home for dinner." He pulled the car keys from his pocket. "At least then you won't have to deal with this tonight. We can hang out at my place."

I nodded.

"Good thing I couldn't get that gun at Jason's, huh? I would've opened up on them."

I nodded again, but part of me liked the idea. Just the idea.

I got cleaned up at Erik's house. His mom was gone, of course, and his dad was hidden away in his office listening to Led Zeppelin, so my battered face made it down into the rec room unnoticed. I cleaned out my scrapes in the bathroom before wandering back into the basement. Erik came down with ice wrapped in a dishtowel.

"Keep your head tilted back," Erik said. "Don't bleed all over the carpet."

"It makes the blood go down my throat." I sounded stuffy and goofy, sitting on the beanbag with the ice to my nose.

"Welcome to Birch Hills, where quality is a way of life." He took off his jacket and tossed it on to the floor. "Hold on, I'll be right back."

Erik hurried back upstairs. I slumped against the wall. My head throbbed and painful specks of light danced across my vision. The room's beige walls and recessed lights made it seem like a spaceship infirmary. I wondered if my brain was bleeding. He plodded back into the room, this time bringing me a couple of white pills and a glass of water. He switched on some droning ambient music, then collapsed into the recliner beside the beanbag.

"I'm sorry you got hurt," he said. "If I'd known you were going to do that, I would've stopped you. Or helped you sooner. Why'd you freak, man? Because of that picture of your dad? Or Lindsay, or what?"

"What?" I coughed. "I don't know. Everything's messed up."

"Yeah. The end is near."

"That, and you're not exactly the most low-stress friend to have."

"What do you mean?"

He looked at me with confusion so earnest and genuine that I wanted to slap him. The first thought in my mind was how Lindsay had been in his bedroom that day, but I didn't want things to end up like they had before, and there wasn't much to say at this point.

"Okay," I said, "well, you keep talking about wanting to carry a gun, for one."

"I don't really mean it. Well, most of the time I don't." He laughed. "Look. What happened to you at Gas-Go has happened to me more times than I want to remember. I got two choices: put up with the suckiness of people in silence or take the beatings for not playing along. It's scary."

"You hide it well."

"Nah. Hate's louder than fear, that's all." He sighed. "I miss my mommy. I'm a big wuss."

"No, you're human. Hate to break it to you. But what does a gun have to do with that?"

"Not much," he said. "I just wish there was something I could do other than be scared all the time."

I swallowed blood. We were underground, and droning music pulsed through the soft gloom.

"Is that what the Doomsday Book is?"

"You looked at it when I left it in your bag, didn't you?" His voice was flat. "You read it."

"I peeked," I said. "I couldn't help it. I'm sorry; it has a great title."

"Okay, I'll buy that. I don't know what you saw, but I'll come clean. I've been meaning to show this to you for a while. I wanted it to be a surprise."

He stood and gestured for me to follow him. I walked, careful to keep my head tilted back. We crossed the rec room to his gaming table. It wasn't laid out in a way I was used to. Gone were the pyramids and castles, the trenches and airstrips, the Viking ships and steampunk dirigibles. Something more earthly had replaced them.

A dull redbrick institutional building covered most of the tabletop. The rest held a parking lot filled with miniature cars, a football field, and a little chunk of Main Street, complete with a library, millpond, and gazebo—all honeycombed with hexagons for troop movement. Erik had made Birch Hills into a battlefield.

But what attention to detail! The gazebo had been assembled from toothpicks and painted white. There was a striped barbershop pole on Main Street, and a bike rack by the park—with bikes. Little tombstones stood in the cemetery. There were trees, sidewalks, and newspaper boxes. Birch Hills High had no roof, so I could see inside. He'd stenciled Eddie Eagle's face onto the floor of the basketball court. He'd included the green benches in the school's courtyard, and made a car up on a lift for the auto shop. Lockers lined the main hallways, painted green in the west wing and gold in the east. I lowered my ice pack.

"Wow. If this were for a model train instead of a miniature battlefield, you'd make the front page of the *Observer*."

I stood there amazed. It seemed strange that Erik would spend so much time recreating something he claimed to hate so much, just so he could play out a fantasy of running amuck through it. He raged against Birch Hills, but he knew it well. It was all he knew. This place had defined him. I suppose it's no surprise he'd spent so much of his time defining it, too.

He smiled as he pulled out a box of little plastic people, and then populated little Birch Hills with cops and kids, teachers and businessmen, firemen and football players; he held each figure between his thumb and forefinger and placed it with care. He set a tiny brown jeep in the Gas-Go's lot and laughed. Then he reached under the table and handed me a small box, the sort used for fishing tackle. I popped it open.

Inside stood rows of soldiers: some futuristic, some medieval, some contemporary, each spattered with red. All had bone-white faces, black clothes, and heavy weapons. The only exception was a row of carefully painted Victorian carolers—the robots that had rebelled.

"Want to play?" he asked. "We can take out the whole place. You'll feel better."

I set the box on the edge of the table and plucked out the miniature street urchin. He didn't have a box of apples, but Erik had taken the time to paint a pair of sunglasses on him.

We played past midnight. There were no survivors. He was right. I felt better.

When I got home, it was about one a.m. I dropped my coat next to the door, kicked off my sneakers, and walked to the bathroom to look for some aspirin. I grabbed a little bottle of Ibuprophin, shook out a couple tablets, and quickly dry-swallowed them.

Dad's old records spun on through the dead of night. Fuzzy guitars and rough voices echoed up from the basement through the air ducts. A voice wailed from the metal vent in the bathroom wall, the blues pouring down like hail.

I trudged upstairs, heading for bed, hoping Dad hadn't heard me come in. Paul's bedroom door seemed to pull me toward it. My swollen hand ached when I reached out and turned the knob.

The room had been closed up for a long time, probably since Christmas; Paul hadn't come home for Easter. When the door swung open, the whole room took a breath, pulling air from the hall around me and the wind from my chest.

I reached around the doorframe and flipped the switch, but the bulb was dead. Light from the hall formed a long, slanting bridge across the floor. When I stepped into the room, my shape cut a black hole down the bridge's center. It looked as though I could fall right through my own shadow.

Everything in the room was unchanged: the mattress, the little toy robots, the posters of jet fighters and galaxies. I thought it was strange how things just stayed in place until someone touched them, like maybe time would stop if nobody were there to perceive it. I remembered several things I'd lost—a nice, green jacket left on the playground, a toy robot at the beach, the cat who ran away when I was nine—and realized how, even if I were to get them back, they would have been changed by absence. Our time apart meant they would become outgrown, unfamiliar, or irrelevant— but I still missed them, and I didn't know why. The jacket would be too small now. I didn't play with toys. I wished Paul were home. I wanted to call Lindsay but didn't know what to say or how to unmake the things that happened. I made my way over to the closet and opened the door on things stored away.

No light from the hallway streamed into its cramped space. I leaned in, reaching blindly, my shins scraping on a plastic storage bin, my arms shoving past old Boy Scout uniforms and Halloween costumes, until my hands finally closed on the air rifle's barrel. I dragged it out, the stock scraping against the wall, and then held it against me.

It was cold and hard. I knew it was just a toy, not a real gun, not something that could kill a person. But it had sure done a number on Chippy the squirrel. It was a smaller version of the real thing.

Dad's footsteps came thudding up from the basement. I shut the closet and leaned the BB gun in the corner when I heard him climbing the next set of stairs. Soon, he stood in the hallway beyond the door, squinting through the dark. His glasses were low on his nose, and gray stubble covered his cheeks and chin. He looked gigantic, his shadow swallowing up the bridge of light, but his face seemed tired and confused.

"Hey, Joshua," he said. "What are you doing?"

"I wanted to borrow some of Paul's comic books."

We whispered like conspirators meeting in the middle of the night.

"Looking for comic books in the dark?"

"The light's burned out."

"Come here a sec, will you?"

I walked slowly, trying to keep by body between him and the air rifle so he wouldn't see it.

"You didn't hang up your coat." He stood over me, tilting his head to one side and peering down at my face. "What happened to you?"

"Nothing." I shrugged. "I got in a fight."

"Let me see."

Dad took my chin between his thumb and forefinger, tilting my head to one side, his hand cool and dry. He turned my head and examined the scrape on my cheek, then turned my face back to him. He leaned forward, looking first in my left eye and then my right. His thumbs pressed gently on either side of my nose. It was sore.

Dad sighed out a gust of beer-stale heat. "I don't think your nose is broken, and if it is, it's not displaced. Did you clean out that scrape already?"

"Yeah," I said, "with Bactine at Erik's house. I know it looks bad, but I got some good hits in, Dad."

"You don't usually get in fights," he grumbled. "What happened?"

I shrugged. "Erik and me always take shit from guys, you know? It's not a big deal. I just lost it today. I just couldn't take it." I looked down at my stocking feet, and his big hand brushed the hair from my forehead. "I usually don't let it get to me, but sometimes I get so pissed, I just want to kill them."

I hadn't meant to say that last part, at least, not that way. I wasn't even being literal or anything. Dad's hand dropped from my face and he took a step back. He opened his mouth to say something and then closed it, pursing his lips together into a thin line. He cleared his throat.

"I know how that can be," he said. "If this keeps happening, I mean, these sorts of problems, come talk to me about it. Okay?"

I nodded. He reached out with both hands and cradled my swollen wrist in his fingers. He lifted it up and then stooped forward to peer at it.

"Don't go to your mother about these kinds of things," he said, examining my scraped knuckles. Dustin's teeth had done that when I hit him. "You usually go to your mother."

I reached back into my pocket with my left hand, and the folded page from the war book was slick against my fingertips. Before I could take it out, Dad stood up and grasped my shoulders so tightly that I almost winced. My face reflected in the lenses of his glasses, twin ghosts superimposed over his eyes. That grin spread across his face, the one that turned down at the corners, and I thought of the shirtless GI with the dead man.

"Be careful out there," he said. "Next time, you're probably better off running."

I nodded again. He tousled my hair, patted me on the shoulder, and told me not to stay up too late. Before shuffling off to bed, he glanced over my shoulder, into the dark. I don't know if he saw the rifle there or not. We stood there for a moment, looking at one another, and neither one of us said a thing.

13

I sat on my bed with the headphones plugged into the amplifier, playing my bass, nodding my head to the rhythm with my eyes closed. A hand on my shoulder made me yelp. Mom, startled, took a big step backwards and bumped into my dresser. My toy Godzilla toppled off it and onto the floor.

"Jesus," I growled. The instrument cable and headphone cord tangled, ensnaring me.

"I called up for you five times, mister," she said. "Erik's downstairs."

"Well, send him up, then," I said.

"I'm not the butler, Joshua. And he said you were coming down to meet him. He's outside." She lowered her voice. "What happened to his car?"

"Huh? What do you mean?" I managed to free myself from my musical equipment. "Be down in a sec."

"That boy needs a shower," she said. "Someone should have a talk with him."

Erik was sitting on the porch when I came out, wearing sunglasses and looking at his Acura. The front end was smashed, the crumpled metal streaked with yellow paint.

"The road gate at Shady Glen," he said.

"What?"

"I didn't stop in time," he said. "Will you walk with me for a second?"

"Yeah, sure."

His boots' hobnails clicked on the pavement as we made our

way down the street. The weather had been nice for more than a week, rare for Michigan in the spring. I knew it would turn soon enough. It always did.

"I need your help with something," he said. "I'm really sorry, but I don't know who else to ask."

In the years I'd known him, Erik had never asked me for help doing anything.

"What's going on?"

"I'm in trouble, man. You have to just help me do this one favor. Then I swear I won't be mixed up with any more of it. Need help 'cause I can't do it now."

He spoke choppily, every little sound and motion around us grabbing his attention. Hedge trimmers, automatic garage doors, lawn sprinklers, all of it.

"Jason and them are gonna beat the shit out of me if I can't get somewhere in the next hour. I mean, bad. But I can't drive right now. I mean, you saw my car. What I did."

"What? Why can't you drive?"

"I'm all messed up on some shit right now. Can't see. My timing's blown. And I forgot I was supposed to drive a package out to some meeting point for Jason and the Farm guys. Just forgot."

"A *package*? Jesus Christ," I snapped. "Why do you have anything to do with that stuff? Are you retarded?"

"After the cops came out looking for Apple Boy, Jason got all paranoid and didn't want to keep shit at the Farm, and Trav didn't want it at the crash pad—"

"Crash pad?"

"You know, the Leatherwolfs Motorcycle Club, and—"

"Oh, my God."

"—And I offered to hold onto it and drive it sometimes, since I live in Shady Glen, and then they'd help me out, too. But I forgot about having to get this shit over to some handoff today. I'm wasted. If I don't make it, they'll beat the shit out of me. Please, I need a driver."

"No," I said. "No way."

"Please, you got to. If I drive myself, I'll crash, or worse, get pulled over and searched, and then I'll be done for."

"No. This isn't my business. You even said so."

"But," he stammered, "but I stood up for you. At the Gas-Go."

Damn it. He had me there. Kids yelled and splashed in someone's backyard swimming pool while we stood looking at each other.

"It's not the same," I said. "At all. You're asking me to help you do something illegal."

"No," he said. "I'm asking you to help me get out of it. After this, I'm done. Please."

"No more visits to the Farm. No more of your wannabe gangster crap."

"I swear. Just this once. Please."

He took off his sunglasses and raised his right hand. His pupils looked like black pennies. A breeze blew, and I got a whiff of his stink, like gym clothes and wet garbage.

"Okay," I said, "fine."

"Thank you, thank you, thank you," he said, handing me the keys. "I owe you."

"Let's just get this over with."

We went back and walked around the car, making sure the turn signals and brake lights worked. I eased the Acura out into the street but spun out when I drove away. The rear-wheel drive had a lot more power than my mom's car. I kept it at exactly two miles over the speed limit.

"You know," he said and then repeated, "You know? That time you said that stuff about my dad?" he said, as I drove around the lake.

"Please don't go there," I answered.

"No, I'm not mad about it. Something about trailer park hot-tubbing. What was that?"

"I was just trying to piss you off," I said.

"I mean, check it out. Like, I know he cheats on her. I told you. But you said—"

"Look, it was just a dickish thing to say." I said. "Which way on Lakewood?"

"Right. No. Left," he said. "Then make a right on Weber Drive."

We made our way into the neighborhood. It was on the other side of Heron Lake, the opposite of the white-gabled McMansions and landscaped lawns in Shady Glen. My dad told me most of these houses were built as cottages for summer rental but had become cheap year-round housing. They were run-down and crappy looking. The place we ended up at was a piss-yellow waterfront ranch. Motorcycles and cars lined the street outside. A few ragged looking dudes in Leatherwolf jackets stood around on the lawn, holding beers. Erik staggered out of the car and pulled a duffle bag from the trunk. He came up and tapped on the driver's side window. I rolled it down.

"I'll wait in the car," I said.

"No, you gotta come. They gotta see you're not somebody they haven't seen."

"Have them look over here," I said, "I'm not—"

"Hey, you two!" Jason had appeared at the door. "Quit fagging around and get your asses moving."

I sighed and got out of the car. We walked up onto the porch. Jason yanked the bag out of Erik's hands.

"Glad you homos could make it," he said, handing the duffel to someone inside we couldn't see. "Whoa. Erik was right; you really did get the shit knocked out of you." He pointed at my black eye and scraped face. "Our man Trav sent those guys a message, so don't you worry about them anymore."

"Um, thanks," I said. "It wasn't that bad."

"Right. Hey, I just got a new boat. We're going to take it out. Come on in. I'll get you dudes some life jackets."

"I really don't think we have time," I said, pointing at my imaginary wristwatch.

"Shut the fuck up and get down to the dock, kid."

We made our way through the house and down to the waterfront. People were crashed out on the couch, drinking on the deck, doing lines in the kitchen, and passing joints on the dock. Many of them I'd seen before, over the winter at the Farm.

Jason's powerboat was one of the bigger kinds, a Bayliner, I think. Amanda was there, too. She'd recently gotten a fake ID so she could work at a strip club near the Detroit airport and wouldn't shut up about it. Kenzie was bombed out of his mind on something or another in the back. Erik and I sat on the side rail in orange life vests, both of us skinny, white, and pale. Jason motored us out, and then we drifted, unanchored in the middle of Heron Lake.

Jason lifted a cylinder the size of a cigarette lighter to his nose and snorted from it.

"Arr, matey," he said, rubbing his left knuckle against his right nostril. "Shiver my timber."

Amanda cackled like a dolphin having a seizure. Erik forced a pained smile. She pranced a couple steps over to Jason and patted his chest. Somehow, a little, turquoise two-piece concealed her broad ass and softball-size breasts. A silver butterfly navel ring sparkled on her taut stomach, and sticky-sweet coconut tanning oil wafted from her. If you were into that sort of look, not that I was, you had to admit she looked kind of good.

Jason paced the length of the boat and back again, his leg-brace squeak-thudding with every step. He'd been through two more surgeries, but his knee (without the brace) still couldn't hold up his weight. As he spent every waking moment drinking beer, snorting drugs, and eating painkillers, I couldn't imagine Jason ever felt much of anything in his bad leg, or anywhere else.

He'd bound up his blonde dreadlocks on top of his head like some sort of crazy samurai helmet, making him seem about seven feet tall. The black lifejacket buckled around his chest looked more like body armor than a flotation device. Amanda stood, leaning against one of the seats. She occasionally lifted a pint of Southern Comfort to her lips or fiddled with her bikini straps as she babbled on about how much work it is to be a dancer.

"What's the worst are the guys who want to *talk*. It's just pathetic, you know? And you have to listen to 'em, too, because that's how it works." She rolled her eyes and took a swig. "And the shoes I gotta wear, ohmigod, don't even get me started…"

And so on. When she spoke, she gestured wildly with pink-taloned fingers—a new addition. I worried someone might lose an eye if she got too excited. Kenzie, in a lime-green polo shirt and cut-offs, slouched in the aft. He ate pistachio nuts from a little plastic bag and tossed the shells over his shoulder. A Hansel and Gretel trail floated on the waves behind. With his sunglasses and headphones on, the guy seemed oblivious to the entire planet around him.

Even though it was colder out on the water, the clear sky and gentle breeze calmed me. Amanda finally stopped talking and rested her head on Jason's shoulder. He placed his arm around her waist. The two of them turned to stand with their backs to Erik and me, silent. Sunlight rippled on the water like liquid gold before them, and they became a postcard. Kenzie stopped munching pistachios by the engine. Waves lapped against the hull, circling seagulls trilled overhead, and distant jet skis buzzed like a beehive. Time stood still in a dazzling moment of sunshine. I was glad to be there.

And then it shattered.

Jason whipped around, pivoting on his good leg, and lashed out his whole arm to point in Erik's face. Erik jerked backwards from the jabbing finger as if it had stung him. Amanda stepped away from her boyfriend, her eyes shining with fear. My insides curdled. I didn't know what Erik had done to piss off his Jason, but he was cornered now. Jason's eyebrows collided into a down-turned arch of blond, and his lips peeled back into a snarl.

"Did you," Jason said in a low, throaty growl, "just ash your cigarette in my boat?"

A strangled laugh tittered from Erik's throat. "What are you talking about? I—I'm not even smoking."

"No shit. Fucker." Jason's nostrils flared, caked with white crust. "Not *anymore* you're not. You think I'm stupid?"

The rocking boat and splashing waves soured in my stomach. My heart punched against my breastbone.

"What?" Erik said. "No, man. I mean, I didn't, I couldn't've ashed, because I, like, you know, I didn't even have a, a—a cigarette. I'm out. You know what I mean? I don't have…I don't *have* any cigarettes. To ash one. I mean."

"Why don't you light up another one, maybe you can ash that

one in my new boat, too. Grind it right out on the seat." Jason smiled. "Go ahead. Do it."

I wanted to do something to help Erik, but I was scared anything I said would make Jason madder. Plus, I didn't want to make myself a target. So I just sat there like a catatonic, still as silence, watching it happen. Amanda stood to my right, the fingertips of each hand pressed against her upper lip. She almost looked like she was praying.

"Honey?" Her voice was tiny, small in a way I never imagined possible for her. "Are you okay? Hon?"

He kept his frying stare locked on Erik. "I'm serious. *Do it.* I'm telling you to do it."

"Jay-boy," Kenzie prattled absently from the back. "No, dude. Dude. No. Jay-boy…"

"I don't have any cigarettes," Erik said quietly.

I'd seen Erik get roughed up plenty of times, but this time I was terrified. Maybe it was because he looked so small sitting there next to me, his arms like white bones poking out from the orange puff of the lifejacket, his narrow hands resting on his knees. The shadow of Jason's bulk swallowed him. Maybe it was because we were stuck in the middle of Heron Lake, with nowhere to run and no one to call for help. Or maybe it was because I had no idea why Jason was angry, or what he wanted to do, or why he was doing it. Like a rabid dog or a zombie, something terrible had happened to his brain, and none of us could hope to put him down.

"I'm not asking you, shithead. I'm telling. Do it," he said.

"Honey." Amanda's voice trembled. "Leave him alone."

"I'm going to count to three," Jason said.

"What the fuck, Jason? *I don't have any cigarettes.*" Erik's voice broke slightly. I hoped that he'd jump overboard if things got bad, so I could jump off, too. But then I wondered if Jason would try to run us over with the boat.

"One," Jason said, raising a finger in front of him.

"Stop it," Amanda said. "I mean it."

"Two."

"You're insane," Erik said. "Come on, please. I'm sorry."

"*Jason!*" Amanda screeched. "Fucking cut it out!"

"Three."

Amanda put herself in front of Erik and threw her arms around Jason, either trying to hug him or to hold him back. A horrible sound came out of her boyfriend, like a choke, a sob, and a howl, all at once, and then his head fell against her smooth, tanned shoulder, his dreadlocks tumbling forward to hide his face. Amanda screamed. Her body thrashed and her long nails dug into his biceps. Jason's hair swung to the side, and I saw what he'd done.

He'd sunk his teeth into her shoulder. His eyes rolled up into his head, half circles of blue gazing up at the sky from beneath the heavy lids. Kenzie's voice flatly barked, "No, hey, hey, no…" Jason jerked his head left and right, and a thin stream of blood oozed from the corner of his mouth, shining like red glass in the sun. Grunting breaths burst in my ears, and I realized they were my own. The engine vapors and the lake's wet murk became a sickening reek. Amanda screeched and flailed, unable to separate her shoulder from his jaws. Then he threw her aside, or she managed to pull free. She tumbled down onto the deck. The whole world sickeningly listed left and right. Pulled off balance, Jason's leg-brace thumped forward. He hunched over with his arms spread wide, his hands clenched into fists, and his chin smeared with blood. A patch of shadow crossed his face. Blue irises gleamed from that darkness and then locked with my own.

I did what came naturally. My stomach was already sloshing and sour from the rocking of the boat and the ratcheting terror, so when Jason stumbled toward me, I threw up.

I vomited magnificently: my jaw dropped and my stomach forced everything out of me. A red-brown chunky jet of puke sprayed into his face. His hands flew up to cover his eyes, his body twisted to my left, and then something knocked him aside. Hard.

Erik had dropped his shoulder and lunged with all of his weight into Jason's bad leg, drilling into the crippled knee. Jason spun and pitched backward, his arms flailing like an osprey trying to take flight, and then he bowled over side-rail. Cool water sprayed across my face as he splashed into the lake.

He coughed and floundered in the water, his voice not angry, but desperate.

"My leg! I can't swim," he screamed. "Help me! I can't swim with my leg! Help!"

Amanda dashed to the side of the boat, weeping, "Oh my God, baby, oh my God!" She made to reach out to him, but Erik, now standing, put his hand on her forearm and firmly pulled it back.

"He has a lifejacket, Amanda," he said. "It'll hold up."

"Oh my God," she said again. "He can't swim. His leg."

"Don't let him back on this boat. Not now. He has a lifejacket."

"What's going on?" Kenzie mumbled to no one. "What the hell, dude. Jay-boy? Dontcha know you can't swim?"

Jason continued to plead and wail. I spit between my feet and wiped my lips with the back of my hand. My mouth tasted like bile and orange juice. My whole body shook.

"He's *not* getting back on the boat," Erik said. "It's not safe right now. You're bleeding."

A dark rose-petal had formed on her shoulder. The hand she had tried to offer Jason reached up, across her body, and touched the wound. She held her white palm in front of her and stared at the smear of red. Jason's screams grew more unintelligible as his splashing continued. Amanda's chin dipped down, and she shook her head.

"Crazy," she whispered, like it was a solemn secret. "This is fuckin' crazy."

"Someone from the house can get him," Erik offered.

"René doesn't like water," she said, distantly.

"I know," he replied. "Maybe Kenzie will do it, once his head clears up a bit."

"I'll do it," he called from the back. "Just tell me what I'm doing, and I'll do it!"

"There," Erik said. "You see?"

"You know what?" She reached back to hold the bite. "This ain't my problem."

"You probably should get out of here once we get back to the house," Erik replied.

She coughed out a laugh. "Really? You think?"

He looked to me and asked, "Do you know how to drive a boat?" but before I could answer, Amanda snapped, "No way. I'll drive."

She sat down in the seat and pulled down on the throttle. The engine purred and gurgled as she made a wide left turn, toward the shore, away from Jason. Erik stood beside her with his arms folded. They both stared dead ahead.

"Baby, help, help me baby," Jason pled. She dropped the lever down again, and the purr became a steady roar. I looked back to see him waving his arms like a shipwrecked man, bobbing in the wake, getting smaller as we motored away.

Kenzie, smiling like he'd won a pageant for head-injury victims, waved back at him.

When we got to shore, Amanda tied up the boat with a sailor's efficiency before stepping out onto the dock. Erik and I followed her, marching down the planks like men trying not to run. We pulled off our lifejackets and dropped them without breaking pace. The odor of the fresh varnish, mixed with the sharpness of cut grass, turned my aching, empty stomach. Kenzie remained in the boat, calling after us, "So, are we just going to leave him out there?"

Amanda marched across the lawn, and Erik followed her. I didn't know why he wasn't heading to the car, but I stayed with him. I hoped to God he wasn't thinking about hooking up with her right now, of all times. He's never been interested in her before, but his head was a mess lately, so it seemed possible.

She stormed up to a big umbrella table, under which René lounged in a folding chair. With him was a guy in a shirt and tie who looked about fifty, and a mohawked chubby girl who looked about fifteen. I didn't recognize the older dude until I spotted the heart-and-dagger tattoo on his forearm. It was the Greek guy from the waffle place.

"Mandy," René said, leaning back and lacing his fingers behind his shaved head. The sleeves of his kimono billowed like a pair of butterfly wings. "What is the problem?"

"Don't call me Mandy," she said. "And you tell your washed-up, crippled friend that he better not ever come near me again," she said.

I poked Erik in the back.

"Let's go," I whispered. He ignored me. The old guy and the punk girl gazed across the lawn or up into the umbrella, making a point of not involving themselves.

René stroked his moustache. "What happened? Jason, he is in one of his moods, yes? Like when he tear off the door?" René lifted his hands, palms up, fingers spread wide. "You know better than to be around his moods."

"He bit me," she said. "That gimpy, roid-head asshole *bit* me."

René looked up at Erik and me. He raised an eyebrow in puzzlement. His moustache twitched before he asked, "Is true?"

"Yeah," we said simultaneously.

"Look," Amanda said, turning her shoulder toward the table to present the wound. Everybody winced. "So I left him out there. You'll have to go get him."

"Oh, no, not me," René said with a wave of his hand.

"You should wash that bite out," the punk girl said.

"No shit," Amanda snapped. The girl looked down at her Converse sneakers. "I'm out of here. And you tell Jason to leave these two guys alone, too. They didn't do anything. Got it?"

René only grunted, and I swear every muscle in Amanda rippled like a bunch of ropes tightening beneath her bronzed skin. "Do you understand?" she said. "If you don't, I'll take it out to the Farm, and there'll be *problems*."

He nodded and held out his hands, "Sure, sure. You go now. Far from here. We will get Jason when you have gone far. It will be all good."

"Um, René, you still selling that gun?" Erik asked.

"The .38? You just missed it, my friend." René laughed. "I sell it to a man an hour ago. To protect his semi truck on the road, he say. What you need a gun for, boy?"

The old Greek smiled at that and patted the chubby girl on the knee. I grabbed Erik by the shoulder and roughly pulled him away as Amanda stomped off.

The three of us walked around the house to the driveway. As we turned the corner, I said, "Amanda, thanks."

She stopped and turned to look at me, one hand on her hip. "For what?"

"For saving Erik from getting his ass kicked."

"Hey," Erik said. "I could've handled it."

"Of course, Erik. You're a man, right? All you guys can handle everything."

She stared out over the lake as she spoke, so I turned to look, too. I could see Jason out there. He seemed like just a shadow of a man, cast away. I worried that a boat or a jet ski might cut him down. I thought that his lifejacket might fail, and the weight of his leg-brace would pull him down to the lake's murky bottom. He was alone, all torn up and stitched back together like Frankenstein's monster. Part of me wanted to go back for him, even after all the craziness. But I knew he'd turn on me, or he'd pull me in there with him. It didn't matter; I didn't even know how to drive a boat.

"I thought he was such a good catch, too," she said. She laughed, a weird kind of hoot, and then rubbed the back of her hand on her mouth. Her jaw clenched, and the whole of her looked hard, angular, and hungry.

"My mom always said this thing about junkyard dogs," she said. "I never got it when he fucked around on me, or smacked me, or when he yelled at me and broke my stuff. He's never going to get any better. Shit. Junkyard dogs. They bite everybody except the ones who raise 'em."

She held up her hand like a woman being sworn in at court, the blood on her hand already drying to a sticky brown.

Erik and I only nodded. My eyes felt kind of watery; maybe the cut grass was bothering my allergies. I pushed up my glasses and stood shifting my weight from one foot to another.

She looked at me, then, and said, "Lindsay really liked you, you know. You were supposed to chase after her. Why's everybody's got to make shit so hard for everybody? You going to try to work it out, or just be like the rest of the assholes?"

I floundered for words and, finding none, only shrugged. Amanda's smile withered me. She walked down the driveway, climbed into her pickup, and drove away.

"I'll drive," Erik said. "My head is all cleared up now."

As we pulled out onto the main road, I said, "What was that about a gun? You promised me you were done with that if I drove us out here."

"Oh, that? I really gotta get one before Y2K hits. After 2000, the world will go bat-shit crazy. I mean, C-R-A to the Z to the double-E, you know?"

"You don't need a gun. You live in Birch Hills."

"No, that's exactly why I need one," he said. "That was some great puking back there, though." He laughed. "Linda Blair's got nothing on you. Wow. That really helped out. You saved my life today. For real. In a week or two, this will all seem funny, I bet."

I just said, "Maybe."

14

ysteria kicked in the following Tuesday. The scrape on my cheekbone from the Gas-Go beating had crusted over into an itchy scab. So far I'd managed not to scratch it. I leaned against Erik's bedroom door after school, fanning my hand in an attempt to clear smoke from the air.

Mike Kahuakai sat cross-legged on the floor, chubby-cheeked and bald-headed. He looked like a freakishly huge baby, passing the bong to Erik and then exhaling another thick plume of smoke. The cloud drifted up to the TV, where news of a high school shooting-spree flashed across the screen. A clip of speeding ambulances and police cars quick-faded to a medium shot of two girls, about our age, clinging to each other and crying. Erik lolled back on his bed, saying, "Hey, the one on the left's pretty hot."

Less than a week after Erik and I played a tabletop wargame in which we slew our hometown population down to the last man, a very real slaughter of a similar nature occurred on the other side of the country. Erik's desire to obtain a handgun, and the fact that his father owned two assault rifles, seemed much more of a dangerous situation than it had before.

Despite all that, I hung out in his bedroom after school. It was the size of my parents' living room, equipped with a TV, a computer, three gaming consoles, a few thousand dollars worth of guitar equipment, and God knows what else buried under the dirty laundry.

Mike and Erik passed the bong back and forth. We all stared up at the murder news on the screen, broadcast live from Colorado.

"...the Sheriff's department has dispatched fire engines to the residence of one of the shooters," the newscaster said, "Seventeen-year-old Eric Harris…"

"Oh shit," Erik said. He tucked the bong between his knees and buried his face in his hands. "His name is Eric, too? Great. I am *sooooo* fucked. Eric. Great."

The TV was calling it "The Columbine High Massacre," which I thought sounded like the name of a direct-to-video slasher movie. Throughout our school day, we'd only heard whispers of the incident. Erik and Mike had been blazing up between classes, because it was April 20, which I guess was like a holiday for potheads. Erik suggested this had something to do with Hitler's birthday. I couldn't tell if he was joking or not.

An eerie and watchful tension had surrounded the teachers and staff, the sort of fear kids can smell. When school let out, cops stood on the sidewalk by the buses, and two police cruisers flanked the student parking lot. Erik gave Mike and me a ride to his place, and that's where we saw how the massacre had taken over every TV channel. It was like a cancer.

"So," I said, sitting next to Erik on the bed, "maybe you shouldn't wear your black trench coat tomorrow."

"The jocks and preps'll think twice about hassling you if you do," Mike laughed.

"Black trench coats should be our new school uniform," Erik said. "The kid you pick on today might be the one pointing a gun at you tomorrow. People need to remember that shit."

Mike Kahuakai had become Erik's new dealer since the run-in on Jason's boat. Those guys had pretty much stayed away from us, and we had avoided them. Kenzie still said hello when we ran into him downtown, but that was it. Lindsay and Amanda stayed tight, and both had kept away from the Farm, from what I'd heard. There were rumors that Li and Lindsay had hooked up at a field party over spring break. Having the three of us together in art class got pretty uncomfortable. We tried to act like everything was normal, all small talk and little jokes, and then dodged each other outside of class. I didn't know if Lindsay and Erik still talked and tried not to care.

Mike was pretty harmless compared to Jason, René, and the old Farm crew. He watched cartoons and made hemp necklaces, and must've had fifty different tie-dye shirts. The one he wore that day read, in big, happy letters, *Another Shitty Day in Paradise*.

"If those psychos had gotten stoned today," Mike said, pointing at the flickering screen, "this wouldn't have happened."

"You think they shot everybody because they didn't smoke pot?" I asked. "That's retarded."

"No, man, no," Mike said as Erik hunched over the bong. "I'm just sayin', if they'd been stoned, they wouldn't have done it."

"Why?"

"Because," Erik spoke up, his voice thin and throaty as he held his hit, "nobody does anything when they're stoned."

Erik loosed his lungs.

Some teenage girl gave a weeping telephone voice-over to an aerial shot of Columbine High. "…And they shot the prayer-circle girl," her static-twinge voice gasped between sobs.

I looked around at the comic-book apocalypse that exploded on Erik's bedroom walls: glossy posters of angry guitarists, leering skulls, and malevolent robots. Suddenly, the news stopped to run a commercial for dandruff shampoo. The commercial insisted life offered no second chances, especially to make first impressions.

"I like to jerk off when I'm stoned," Mike said.

"What?" Erik stared at him. "Dude, no. What's the matter with you?"

"I don't mean I want to *right now*." Mike said. "You said nobody does anything when they're stoned. I like to jerk off, though. When I get high."

"We all do, Mike." Erik shook his head. "We just don't *talk* about it."

Mike giggled.

The computer-graphic title for the massacre flashed on the screen, and the show started back up again, babbling something about the Internet and "gothic subculture."

"…but there is one question haunting all of us," the newscaster said in her practiced voice of concern. "How could this happen?"

Erik laughed, twisting his fingers in his hair and rocking back and forth.

"How could this happen?" He shouted back at the screen. "How could this happen? You stupid bitch. The real question is, 'Why did it take so long for this to happen!'"

He snatched the remote control from the nightstand, jabbed its off button, and then hurled it across the room. I winced as it cracked against a poster of Doctor Strange, sending the batteries in all directions.

Erik's widened pupils turned his eyes a gleaming black. His chin lowered to his chest, as if he were an animal about to pounce.

"Relax, man," Mike said, smiling. "It's okay. We just have to deal. We're all trapped like the puma in the basement."

I asked Mike, "Is that some sort of Hawaiian saying or something?"

"Nope," he said. "At my house, we have a puma in our basement. It's really a bummer."

"Bullshit," Erik said. "I'm not in the mood for this."

"The tragedy's really getting to you, huh?" I said.

"Yeah. Let's have a moment of silence for the all poor, dead jocks."

"Man, murdering people is wrong," Mike said. "But this puma—"

"Shut up." Erik sighed. "You don't have a lion at your house."

"It's a puma," Mike said.

"A puma is a sort of lion," I clarified. "A puma and a mountain lion are the same thing."

"Cougars and panthers, too." Mike nodded.

"Cougar, puma, whatever. You don't have one."

"You want to see it?"

Glaring at Mike, Erik leaned over him and said, "Yes, as a matter of fact, I do. Show me the puma, baby."

Mike shrugged. "Okay, let's go. My dad won't be back till late."

"Lemme finish this first," Erik said.

He lifted the bong, an onyx-colored acrylic tube with the word STORMBRINGER printed in red letters down one side. Once he'd cashed it out, he stood up, dragged open his closet door, and stepped inside. After some noisy rummaging, he emerged wearing a wrinkled black trench coat.

"Oh, come on," I said. "You're not wearing that thing *today*, are you?"

He walked to the mirror beside the bedroom door and then brushed a few flakes of dandruff from his shoulders.

"Let's roll," he said.

We crept down the massive curving staircase that led to what his mother used to call the "great room," our stocking feet padding gently on the dark burnished wood. The smell of lemon furniture polish became an acrid taste in the back of my throat. As we neared the bottom of the stairs, I heard music; this time it was some old guitar-rock I didn't recognize.

"Dammit," Erik muttered. "Dad's in his office. Try to keep it down."

As we made our way past the leather couches and glass tables, heading to the front hall and foyer, Mr. Grundler called from one of the doorways behind us.

"Erik?"

He froze and called back over his shoulder, "Whattup, Dad?" and then pointedly rolled his eyes at Mike and me.

"If you and your friends are going to smoke in the house, please use the air filter." I couldn't see him at all from the great room, the half-closed door only revealing a strip of beige wall. "I gave the filter to you for a reason."

"I'm sorry, *okay*?" Erik said. "I was just a bit distracted 'cause of the massacre and stuff."

"Quite a story, isn't it?" The rock music sang something about California. "You kids today, eh? Perhaps the world *does* end with a bang. Where are you all off to?"

"We're going to see a puma."

Mike poked Erik in the ribs, mouthing the words "Don't tell." Erik waved him off.

"Great, great. You boys have fun," Erik's dad called back. "Don't go shooting up your Student Council or anything."

"No way," Erik said. "It's too trendy now."

Erik's dad exploded with laughter, and we made our way out the front door. As the three of us strolled past the yipping dogs and whirring hedge-trimmers in the Shady Glen Community of Birch Hills, among the shadows of gabled roofs and three-car garages, the air was cool and damp with springtime. I knew the massacre was playing on every TV set in those big, new houses. I imagined eyes at every window staring at us.

How did we look to them? Humming cheerfully and kicking loose pebbles in the street, Mike led the way. Erik followed, and I walked beside him with my hands buried in my coat pockets.

I always assumed people would take me as a shy arty-poet type, a gangly teenager with purple hair, thick glasses, and funny clothes. Quiet. Watchful. Now, after the massacre, they'd probably see me as potential sniper. Fear made people stupid. I worried that Bigmart might not hire me back to bag groceries over the summer.

Erik walked with his head down, his eyes red slits and his mouth an unwavering grimace. His black trench coat billowed in the wind. We'd both been picked on, hassled, and beaten up during our time at Birch Hills High. My eye socket was still dark and my face still scraped from the battering I'd taken at Gas-Go. But I couldn't see the massacre as anything other than twisted, horrible madness. Though he hadn't said it directly, I thought Erik believed those dead kids in Colorado probably had it coming, maybe just for existing in the first place.

"Your dad seems pretty alright," Mike said to him, now skipping along a few steps ahead of us.

"Yeah. He doesn't give a fuck, you know?" Erik flicked his cigarette butt far across a rolling landscaped lawn. Then he added, absently, "This place used to be an artist's commune."

I yawned as Erik gave a Birch Hills history lesson.

"No shit?" Mike said. "Cool."

"My dad bought it up from one of his friends when it folded. He made a bundle selling to developers."

"Lucky you," Mike said.

"Lucky *him*," Erik corrected.

Brick planters of budding marigolds flanked the Shady Glen Community's gate. It looked like the gayest military checkpoint ever. We formed a Congo line and laughed as we limboed under the bee-striped arms that blocked the road.

The gate arm was bent outward from when Erik had run his car into it trying to get out of Shady Glen. A few days after that, he'd spray painted the whole front of the unmanned guardhouse with a warning: "ABANDON ALL HOPE." The developers had responded to this vandalism by throwing up a fresh coat of paint and installing a security camera. Since the guardhouse was just for looks, I assumed the camera was fake, too.

We walked up to Mike's house, an expansive ranch home fronted with a stone façade. Raked but never bagged, piles of wet leaves from last fall filled the roadside ditch. The open mailbox overflowed with shopping circulars and junk mail.

"I bet the neighborhood association loves you guys," Erik said.

Mike led us around the back of the house, our shoes squinching in the mud. The backyard had a deck, which would've been nice if not for the giant downed tree limb lying across it. It had toppled the grill, which had vomited out wet charcoal briquettes every which way.

Beside the deck was a dented, white aluminum door. Mike pulled what looked like a jailer's ring of keys from his pocket and went about unlatching its four separate locks. Erik stood with his hands on his hips. At last, Mike swung it open and gestured for us to follow him.

We stepped into a small, white laundry room. Over the washer and dryer hung a faded portrait of what was either Jesus or one of the Allman Brothers. Sneakers and boots lay piled in the corner. A door to the left led into the house, but Mike trundled across the room to a different one. His jailer's keyring jingled as he turned yet more locks, whistling. The door at last swung open, revealing a dark basement stairway. A boggy heat blew across the room.

"Fan over the stairs is broken," Mike said, as if this explained everything. "We still gotta fix it. Come on."

Mike clomped down the stairs. Erik gave me a "let's go" head nod and followed. I was glad to be the one closest to the exit. The narrow stairway was a concrete throat, moist and hot, swallowing us. Why was it so warm down there? For the puma? But pumas didn't live in jungle climates. At least, I didn't think they had to.

I took a deep breath as we descended, each wooden step groaning under our weight. I knew I was overreacting. There probably wasn't a puma in Mike's basement, at least not a real one. Looking down at Erik's dark shape in front of me, I remembered how many bong-rips he'd taken before we left and wondered how he was dealing with all of this.

Cobwebbed light bulbs in round yellow cages hung from the rafters of a dingy unfinished basement. Several unseen fans whirred in an undulating drone. The greenhouse air dampened my lungs, and I coughed. To my right, a floor-to-ceiling curtain of black plastic ran the length of the room. The swampy stink of marijuana made it obvious what Mike's dad grew behind it. But there was another scent: the sharp reek of animal, musky and thick. I looked left, and I saw the beast.

A wall of metal bars cut across the basement, making a large cell out of the other side. A gashed and clawed tire hung from the ceiling by a rope. Beside a metal mixing bowl of raw meat was a huge pile of straw. On that straw slept a puma, the color of cinnamon, stretched out on its side like a slumbering convict. My heart stopped. It opened its yellow eyes and returned my stare with indifference. The puma yawned, its pink tongue rolling out from beneath its dagger-sized fangs.

"Oh my dear fucking God," Erik said.

"Bummer, huh?" Mike shook his head.

I felt a little sick when I thought of the puma spending its life locked up underground. I couldn't wrap my head around why someone would do that to an animal, or how in the hell they took care of it. I didn't see a huge litter box—was it housebroken? Did they walk it around the backyard in the middle of the night? How did they control it?

Erik crept over to the bars and knelt down, cooing, "Hey, buddy. Hello."

"Um, Erik," I whispered, "I don't think that's the best idea."

The giant cat lifted and tilted its head. One of the ears twitched as it looked at Erik. Then it flopped back down on the straw, sighed, and closed its eyes. Erik stood up and turned away from the puma's cage. His lips thinned, and lines formed under the corners of his mouth.

"What the fuck, Mike?" His voice was taut. "What's it doing down here?"

"We used to let it wander around the house," Mike explained, "but it ate our ferrets."

Erik huffed out a bitter chuckle. "Of course it did." He stomped over to Mike, grabbed him by the shoulders, and roughly shook him. "I mean, how'd it get here in the *first place*? This isn't right, dude."

Mike stood unfazed in Erik's grip. "I know, man. It's my dad's. I think he traded a few hash bricks and a pot-bellied pig for it."

"So he got the thing and then just put in a cell?" I asked.

Mike shrugged. "Nobody else wants it. He's afraid of people poking around here if he gave it to the zoo or whatever. I think you can figure out why he doesn't want to attract attention to himself."

Erik let go of Mike and then turned back to the puma.

"If I called Animal Control," Mike said, "they wouldn't just take away the puma. They'd take away my dad, too. If I lost him, man, I don't know what they'd do with me."

We all stood silently for a while among the whirring fans. I wanted to pet the puma, but was too scared of it to try. A trickle of sweat ran down the back of my neck. At last Mike said, "Please don't tell anyone, guys."

Erik ground the heels of his hands against his temples. I'd seen him drunk, high, hallucinating, depressed, manic, and in a hundred other states of weirdness, but I'd never seen him like this before—unable to speak or move. He clutched his head and stared at the animal behind the bars. He wrapped his trench coat around himself and turned back to Mike.

"All right," he said, softly. "Fine." He spun on his heel, breezed past me, and clambered up the stairs. The door above screeched open. The bang of its slamming shut struck me in the chest.

Mike looked over to me, folded his hands on his belly, and said, "You won't tell, will you?"

I shook my head. "I should catch up with him, though. I'll see you around."

"It's not how I want things to be, you know," Mike said as I climbed the first step. I paused and looked over my shoulder. The puma had stood up and pressed its massive head against the bars. Mike stooped over and scratched it between the ears. "It's just how things are."

I said, "I'm sorry," and then hurried outside.

I'm not sure what I meant by "I'm sorry." Sorry that his dad was a suburban pot-grower with a giant carnivore locked in his basement? Sorry the puma was serving hard time for nothing other than being out-of-place? Sorry Mike had to deal with things that nobody saw, and if he turned out to be a freak, he'd be the one who'd pay for it? Sorry I had to leave right then, because I was better friends with someone else? I'm sorry. It just seemed like the thing to say, and I don't know why.

I knew Erik was going to Arthur's Pond, because that's where he always went to brood. I ran down the muddy trail, grackles cackling in the budding trees overhead, chipmunks darting through the tangled scrub beneath. When I emerged, breathless, to the ravine's edge, I saw Erik—but I didn't see Arthur's Pond.

The trees had been cut down and laid in mountainous heaps, like the corpses of giants. Huge piles of bulldozed dirt scattered across the ravine floor, and the rest was a flat, brown plain. Scores of little markers had been pushed into the ground. Yellow and red ribbons ran between them, as though a lunatic had sutured up the earth. On the far end of the clearing, a large gash of construction road headed up the hill and vanished behind the trees. A yellow earthmover, the size of an Abrams tank, sat in profile at center. It was unmanned, its massive scoop-shovel lifted in a frozen posture of victory. A house the size of an airplane hangar, its walls without siding and its window panes still wearing the manufacturer's stickers, towered over this desolation.

Erik, a dark, slumped shape, sat atop one of the bulldozer's treads. He gazed about the waste, helpless and small against that machine's form. A tree branch, the length and thickness of a baseball bat, lay across his lap. A few green leaves still sprouted from it. I guessed it was all that he could salvage.

Subdivisions rose up quickly. In a few months, there would be asphalt streets named after trees and animals. Soon after that, the skeletons of house frames, and then the McMansions with Chemlawns and SUVs and swimming pools. This was inevitable.

There was no sign of Arthur's Pond. It was as though it never had been there at all.

Erik threw the branch to the ground, then stood up and climbed into the bulldozer's cab. As he settled into the seat, a huge smile spread across his face. He reached forward and made a twisting motion. After a brief bit of rumbling, the engine turned over and roared to life. They'd left the key in the ignition.

"Wait," I yelled. "Think about it."

Maybe he didn't hear me, or maybe he ignored me. I guessed he'd been thinking about something like this for years, anyway. He pulled on the levers like a mad scientist. The scoop lowered, some gears clattered and ground, and then the monstrosity lumbered forward. It crashed into the house, collapsing the wall and part of the second floor in an avalanche of noise. My ribs ached, and I struggled to breathe. It took me a moment to realize I was laughing.

I had no thoughts when I grabbed up a fist-sized rock and hurled it. It sailed like a buzz bomb, arching high but dropping fast, and the picture window it shattered fell into shards of a reflected world. I ran down into the pit to join my friend, howling, rushing to destroy that house before anyone dared call it a home.

15

The flyers offering a reward for our capture went up the very next day, posted in every supermarket and drugstore breezeway, taped to every downtown lamppost, and otherwise plastered on every available surface in Birch Hills. I was terrified.

I'd never thought that I, a winner of the Rotary Club Good Citizen Award with above-average grades, would ever be a wanted criminal. I imagined CSI forensic investigators running whatever prints they'd gathered into a vast database, causing my driver's photo to pop up on the screen. The feds would take in my crooked glasses and the zit on my chin, nodding with satisfied contempt. Nightmares assailed me, visions of helmeted and masked agents bursting into my bedroom and dragging me away as my sister wailed, my brother laughed, and my parents looked on with acute disappointment. I thought I might carry that fear around inside me forever.

Erik and I hung out at the boat launch at Heron Lake after school. It was a wet and warm Thursday in April, two days after the shootings in Colorado. We sat on a picnic table and looked at the sun on the water. Cottonwood seeds drifted through the air like dreamy snowflakes, and green leaves had unfurled in the trees. The world reeked of sensuality.

Erik held a copy of the wanted flyer in front of him, reading it as if it were a medieval proclamation.

"$1,000 REWARD," he announced, "for information regarding vandalism and worker endangerment in the Shady Glen development..."

He continued on with his bad Renaissance Faire accent and theatrical gestures. Criminals had made unauthorized use of construction equipment to destroy an unfinished residential home. Anyone with information leading to an arrest would receive the reward, no questions asked. The flyer pointed out that the incident had occurred on "April 20, the exact day of the tragedy in Littleton, Colorado," as if the two horrors were inexorably linked to one another.

"A bounty, Josh. For the Marilyn Manson-loving teenage Internet junkies who have come to tear down suburban homes in the name of Satan. Birch Hills is no longer safe." He crumpled the flyer and shoved it into the breast pocket of his leather jacket. "Maybe I should turn myself in and collect."

"Shhhhh." I looked around, scanning the area for any eavesdroppers. "We shouldn't talk about that."

"Relax. Nobody's here. And nobody knows anything."

"What about, you know," I lowered my voice, "*trace evidence?*"

"Are you serious?" He snorted. "Look. The system has its head up its ass. I mean, they're still trying to find *Nazis,* for God's sake. They only have you *believing* they're in control."

"So what are we supposed to do?"

"Don't talk to anyone about it," he said, "and don't be afraid."

He lit up a joint. The air was a stew of pollen and sunbeams and hard for me to breathe. I looked over at Erik, and I hated him.

I hated him for being so happy to hate things, for not caring if he succeeded or failed at school, if he won or lost his battles, and for his easy cheerful contempt of anyone with power. And, most of all, I hated him because all these things were also what drew me to him—and a good number of other people, too. Like Lindsay.

Besides all that, I was a bit scared of him, too. I'd seen his temper become increasingly violent and unpredictable. He'd slid into whatever bad juju Jason and René were running at the Farm without much effort. The sort of scenario Erik had planned out in the Doomsday Book and constructed as a tabletop game suddenly seemed whole lot more malevolent after it played out in reality, even way out west. Part of me wondered if, like a misdirected voodoo doll, the game had made it happen. Even though we never spoke about it, I got the sense that maybe he thought the same thing.

"Hey." Erik poked me in the shoulder and then blew a cloud of weed smoke in my face when I turned. "Relax. This'll all blow over. Some rich asshole will kill his wife or we'll bomb a new country and then everybody will forget about it. We're no threat to anybody."

The following Monday, we were handed the new "Student Safety Guide" in our homeroom. The tri-folded pamphlet detailed all of the things officially banned in the new "Conflict-Free Safe Zone" that was Birch Hills High. Expressly forbidden were the portrayal of violent acts in writing or artwork, and all forms of threatening speech. The dress code now specifically outlawed the wearing of bandanas, gang or occult symbols, studded or spiked jewelry, trench coats, military gear, wallet chains, or any other items that could encourage an environment hostile to learning and security.

"What if it's raining?" Erik asked from his desk in the corner. "I can't wear my trench coat if it's raining out?"

"Get an umbrella," Mr. Hartigan growled.

"What if it's a yellow raincoat, like the Gorton's fisherman wears?"

A few kids laughed.

"A slicker," I offered. "Is a slicker considered a trench coat? And what exactly is an 'occult symbol?'"

"A lot of people worship a Jewish zombie," Erik said.

"Get rid of the goddamn football team if you want to make a less hostile environment," Pink Dick said.

"Richard," the teacher snapped. "Language."

"Freaks like you that brought this on yourselves, cat-killer," Ashleigh said, her blue eyes bright and angry.

Pink Dick shot to his feet behind his desk, and the color ran right out of her. Dustin Lake, my gay-hating parking lot assailant, stood up behind Ashleigh and took a step toward Pink Dick.

"That's enough," Hartigan yelled, rushing between them. "Sit down, people! Sit down! Now!"

Everyone froze, but neither the albino burnout nor the varsity tackle sat down.

Dick's red gaze narrowed behind his glasses. He quietly and evenly explained to Ashleigh and Dustin, "I'm glad they shot people like you at that school. People like you don't get shot *enough*."

Pick Dick leaned forward and spat a loogie onto the student safety pamphlet. He breezed out of the classroom, long, white hair flowing behind him. I was pretty sure today would be the last time he'd ever set foot in one.

Ashleigh started to cry, and Dustin put his arm around her, shouting over the hubub, "You all heard that, right? You heard him. He's expelled, right? Mr. Hartigan, he's expelled?"

Ashleigh wiped the corners of her eyes, saying, "He is *so* expelled."

"Dick would never go on a rampage," Erik said. "He prefers to capture and torture his victims."

I meowed.

"You think you're so cool," Ashleigh seethed at him. "But you're not. You're not cool with anyone who *matters!*"

"Twat? I cunt hear you." Erik cupped his hand to his ear. "Who's cool?"

"*Shut up, all of you!*" Hartigan blew up like a car bomb, silencing the room. His face empurpled, and a vein pulsed in his forehead. "The next person who says a word will be expelled. *Expelled!*"

Erik groaned and put his head down on his desk.

After third hour let out, right before Group A Lunch, Lindsay drifted up to my locker. She was wearing a little pleather miniskirt, black-and-white striped leggings, and an old Rainbow Brite T-shirt meant for an eight-year-old. She'd cut off the shirtsleeves with a razor and used black marker to X-out Rainbow Brite's eyes.

"Josh," she said. "That day I was over at his house, it wasn't what it looked like. I swear."

"You still lied to me about it." I threw my backpack into my locker and slammed it shut.

"Will you grow up? I need to talk to you." Her voice lowered and she said, "We have to get out of here before they come for us."

I turned to look at her. "I don't have time for your spooky-ass crap, Lindsay. Things are messed up enough as it is—"

"They arrested Pink Dick," she said. "And they opened up Erik's locker. They took his sketchbooks and journal. His CDs, too."

"What?" I said. "That's crazy. They can't do that."

"They can do whatever they want."

"You even talk like him."

"Just listen for a sec." She sighed. "Erik already split when he heard they were going through his locker. He's going to pick me and you up at Smoker's Corner in half an hour, then head out to the cabin."

"Cabin?"

"His uncle has a cabin up by Traverse City. We can stay there till stuff chills out. We got to go."

"No." I turned and walked away.

She reached out and grabbed my arm by the elbow, right below the end of my sleeve. She held on, gentle, but certain not to let go. Her touch froze me. I looked back at her and saw something in her wide eyes and slightly parted lips I'd never seen in her before. She was afraid.

"What the hell, Lindsay? He's not our boss. Or our leader." I pulled away from her.

"They're going to try to put us away if we don't—"

"Jeez! You're all making this into some MTV drama bullshit. News alert: Nobody cares about us. You're making this worse by weirding out and ditching school. Stay here with me. Don't go off the deep end with him," I said. "Please. Listen. I know things got messed up. I don't know what I'm doing a lot of time, and I just wanted you to know that I've never had anything like what I had with you, because, I don't know. I love you. I just do. Please don't go."

Her face softened, and she took a step closer to me.

"Josh," she said, reaching for my hands, "you can come with us."

"Nope." I stepped away. "Go play victim with your fuck-buddy. I'm not playing along."

She winced. The slightest tremble in her lower lip wilted my insides.

"Linds, look, I'm just saying—"

"You're not nice, Josh." She grimaced. "I thought you were, but I was wrong."

"What? *I'm* not nice?"

The bell rang. Lindsay said, "I tried," before she joined the stream of tardy students heading down to the east wing. I watched the back of her red head fade into the crowd like a rose petal carried out to sea.

I wish I'd listened to her. Looking back on it, I should have seen it coming.

This is what I know. The hunt began when Richard "Pink Dick" McCreech (albino, longhair, alleged cat-killer) made what were considered threatening remarks to Ashleigh Baer (Student Council Secretary, homecoming court, and all-around hottie) and Dustin Lake (cut-and-tanned varsity tackle with awesome Jeep). He also expectorated onto a copy of the recently issued Birch Hills High Student Safety Guide. Pink Dick then left campus on foot. Mr. Hartigan informed Principal Langley, who alerted the local police of Dick's remarks, in accordance with new safety initiatives enacted after the school shooting in Littleton, Colorado.

They arrested Pink Dick at gunpoint in the local Quickmart while he attempted to buy an issue of *Guitar World* featuring Zakk Wylde on the cover. Dick didn't resist, other than calling the cops "a bunch of gun-crazy fuckwits," which was probably his honest (if unkind) evaluation of them at the time.

A follow-up call from the police to the school resulted in the searching of several lockers, all occupied by Dick's "known associates," or rather, his friends. First on the list was Erik Grundler (known miscreant and drug user on the Advanced Placement course track). Several items in Erik's locker proved to be of interest to the police.

The search of Erik's locker didn't go unnoticed, however. Tommy "Chigger" Li (freestyle rapper, illegal street racer, associate member of the Ca$h Flo Kings) happened to be avoiding gym class with a forged hall pass that morning. He spotted the authorities rifling through Erik's stuff and called his cell phone.

Erik, in turn, attempted to call Josh Reilly (me, just another art-fag trying to survive until graduation in June), but my phone was off (in accordance with school regulations). He then called Lindsay Kruthers and insisted she get me to leave school with her. I refused.

Erik didn't show up for his next class, so the police came up empty-handed when they went there to nab him. Lindsay Kruthers, Tommy Li, Mike "Buddha" Kahuakai, and Dylan "Twitch" Lipinski had all left school upon hearing of a police crackdown and random searches. Birch Hills High was placed in a state of emergency lockdown. No one was allowed to enter or leave the building, and plainclothes cops were posted at every door.

Less than an hour after I watched Lindsay storm away, the police were actively hunting down nearly all of my friends. At that time, only two suspects were in custody. The first was Pink Dick. The other was me.

It was my first time in Principal Langley's office. I never expected to find myself summoned there, much less under the escort of two security guards, but nothing made much sense lately.

I slouched in the chair, tapping my feet and fidgeting. A framed Michigan State hockey jersey hung, slightly off-center, on the wall behind Langley's huge desk. A pair of mutant-looking rubber plants entangled on his windowsill, frozen in battle for sunlight from the courtyard beyond. I looked over my shoulder, through the glass wall, into the reception area. Langley stood talking with a broad-shouldered man in a tan sport coat. The big, older guy looked like a bouncer, or a bodyguard, or an ex-linebacker, the sort of dude who looked stupid shoved into a jacket and tie, no matter how smart he was.

I thought of the cartoon gorilla in a tuxedo from *Who Framed Roger Rabbit?*, the one the detective looks at and says, "Nice monkey-suit." Then it dawned on me that the guy was probably a cop. A bad taste spilled up into my mouth when the two of them walked into the room together.

"Detective Edgars, this is Joshua Reilly." Langley stepped around his desk and gave me a tight-lipped smile as he sat down.

"Well, hey there, slick." The cop thrust his hand out for me to shake, which I reflexively took. His grip was firm but not crushing. He gave it three good pumps and then eased into a seat beside me. "Principal Langley tells me you won the Rotary Club Good Citizen Award."

"Yeah, in, like, ninth grade," I said. "It was an essay contest."

"Josh is going to be a famous writer," Langley said. "Like Stephen King."

"Is that right?" The cop grinned. "My wife loves that stuff. Me, I'm more of a Tom Clancy man. You ever read Tom Clancy?"

I shook my head. The cop looked disappointed. Then I added, "But I liked those movies. The Harrison Ford ones," and he brightened up a bit.

"Yump. He made a great Jack Ryan. Jack Ryan, now there's a real go-getter, eh?"

The cop laughed and slapped me on the shoulder, startling me. I forced a smile. He seemed nice enough. Like one of my uncles who tried to talk to me about football and feigned interest in the fact that I played bass.

"Am I in trouble?" I asked.

"Now, you see, I don't think so." The cop looked over to Langley, who nodded. "Principal Langley says your teachers all think pretty highly of you, and you seem like a good kid to me. I see a difference between you and some of the people you've been running around with, you see?"

I nodded, even though I didn't follow.

He continued, "I was buddies with plenty of troublemakers back in my day, too. Out in Detroit, back before the riots. Soaping windows, TP'ing houses. You know what I mean?"

"I guess."

"But listen, I know times change. Now, they burn down half that city on Devil's Night. Some prank, eh? Things ain't what they used to be." He leaned toward me with his hands on his knees. "You think of yourself as a good person, Josh?"

"Yeah, I think." I looked away from his soft colorless eyes. "I mean, I try to be."

"Sure, sure. I think you are, too. But it seems like you've gotten mixed up in some bad things." He tilted his head. "Looks like you got a bit of a shiner, there. Somebody knock you in the eye?"

"Fell off my skateboard."

"Uh-huh. See, that's not what I heard. But we'll get back to that. You know why so many of your buddies skipped out on school today?"

"Our security guards will let you out if you give them cigarettes."

Langley reddened. The cop nodded.

"Now, that tells me how, but I asked why."

"Dunno." I shrugged. "I didn't go with them."

"Were they planning something?"

"No."

He kept looking at me as if waiting for me to finish my sentence. I added, "They were probably mad about the safety guide. And about Dick getting in trouble."

He didn't look away. I started to sweat a little. The phones in the front office rang steadily. It sounded like a telethon.

"What?" I asked, a twinge of annoyance seeping into my voice.

"Don't act like I'm against you, Josh. You and me, we're good people. I'm just trying to get a handle on what's going on." He shifted his bulk in his chair. "Now, what's this I hear about you getting into street fights?"

I almost laughed at the thought of myself as a "street fighter."

"I'm not joking, son. Word 'round the campfire is that you threw a bottle at a young man's car last week, and then you attacked him when he stepped out to look at the damage."

"What? A bottle?" I was jolted by the accusation, first scared, but then indignant. I was the bad guy in that situation? And he didn't even have his facts right. "That's not what happened. At all."

"Okay, sorry if I got that wrong. No bottle." He chuckled. "But you're saying you did throw something, though."

I needed to shut up.

"Look, kids get in scrapes." He waved away the problem. "I just want to get the story straight. I heard a bottle, that's all I'm saying."

"It was a pink Freezie," I said, quietly. "They were calling me and Erik names. Like they always do. I just got tired of it."

"Is that why you attacked the boy when he got out? Because he picked on you?"

"No, listen. It wasn't like I just attacked him. He said he was going to kill me. All of his friends got out. They've beaten up lots of people. Erik a few times."

"I see." The cop nodded. "Now Erik, he's the one who threatened them with Mace."

"Air freshener," I said.

"How's that?"

"Nothing. Look, I'm the one who got beaten up. What's going on?"

"You know Dustin's dog, the boy with the jeep, I mean, his dog was poisoned. Someone dumped a heap of hog guts on his front porch, too."

"What?" I stammered. "No, I never heard that."

Erik might have put them up to it, but I bet that was the Farm crew's doing. I sure as hell wasn't going to bring them into the conversation.

"Your buddy Erik, he's a troubled kid, eh?"

"Just a kid."

"Into a lot of the gothic stuff. Devil worship, serial killers, things like that."

I smirked despite myself. Erik hated the term "gothic," and would rather listen to At the Gates over Sisters of Mercy any day, but I didn't think Detective Edgars would appreciate a lesson in sub-cultural literacy.

The cop opened up his briefcase and held up a burned CD. It had been labeled in black Sharpie with Erik's jagged handwriting: *MUSIC FOR KILLING*. My stomach sank. Lindsay was right; they'd opened up his locker.

"Oh, come on," I said. "It's not like he's serious about it."

"That's just the start of it," he said. "Your buddy had a whole mess of books about weapons, Nazis, all kinds of crazy stuff. But more that, I'd like to ask you about this."

The cop held up Erik's Doomsday Book.

"It's full of maps of the school," the cop said. "And honestly, it doesn't look good. Things like 'crossfire tables' and 'kill zones.' What's the story?"

"It's just for a game. He builds models and paints them." I tried to speak but nothing came out. "A game," I finally said.

"What's this game called?"

I faltered. After a moment I said, "AGB."

"What's that stand for?"

I shrugged.

"Answer the question, Joshua," Langley said.

The cop glared at Langley, who sheepishly turned to look out his window.

"Josh," said the cop, "ever hear the phrase 'He who is without sin is without fear'?"

"Yeah."

"I need to know this. It'll all come out in the wash later, anyway you look at it."

"All Guns Blazing," I said. "It's a wargame."

"And he wanted to play it here in the school?"

"No." I said. "No, you don't get it. It was just a joke. He built a model of the school." My hands shook, so I put them in my pockets.

"You ever see this model?"

I nodded.

"Son, now I need you to listen to me. I'm not saying things are one way or another. But what if, just let's say what if, it was just a set-up for the real thing?"

"It's not," I said.

"What makes you so sure?" he said. "How well do you really know Erik? Or anyone, really?"

I thought of Mr. Grundler in the hot tub. Of Lindsay's purse hanging on Erik's banister as he came downstairs, buttoning up his shirt. Of Jason sinking his teeth into Amanda's shoulder. I thought of my dad with the gun on his hip, standing on the dead man. Of Erik, picking up the rock to bash me.

"He's not like that," I said.

"I know you think so," the cop said. He patted me on the arm. "And you're probably right. But, son, what if you're wrong?"

He reached into his pocket and handed me a piece of paper. I unfolded it.

$1,000 REWARD, it read, *for information regarding vandalism and worker endangerment in the Shady Glen development…*

The cop said, "I think you've gotten yourself into a place you don't belong. This is your chance to get out of it and make things right."

My chest tightened. Horror rotted my insides and crawled under my skin. I couldn't breathe. He had me. I was done for. All the hours I'd spent studying for tests, working on projects, and trying to stay off drugs and be good despite my so-called "crowd" were gone. My ACT scores, Good Citizen Award, letters of recommendation, and college acceptances, all for nothing. Taken away in a blink. I was caught. I was going to be a Bad Guy.

"Good people lose their way, sometimes," the cop said, sounding like a sad old cowboy and a wise grandfather rolled into one. "You think it's a game, but you know that game's changed. Kids killing teachers, killing one another. I'm not here to pin anything on you. But if you care about your buddy, and about anyone at this school, I need you to tell me anything he might've said about hurting anyone. I need you to tell me where we might find him. Because if he's not on the level, neither of us wants to live with letting something bad happen. And I'm sure you don't want to find yourself wrapped up in the wrong side of this."

My face burned and tears welled up. Rather than let them come flooding out, I talked.

I told them about how he built the warzone on his table. And even that he'd once shown me his dad's assault rifles and had tried a couple times to buy a gun. And how he and Lindsay had taken off to go to his uncle's cabin. I left out anything about the Farm. I didn't say anything about the house we messed up, either. I didn't want connect myself to him at all—even though he'd been the person I'd been most connected to for years.

The cop patted me on the back and didn't ask about the house at Arthur's Pond. Langley told me what a "good student and friend" I'd been, and how "brave" it was of me to turn Erik in. I'd made it back into the Good Guy Club. And I actually felt decent about it, too.

The door clicked open, and I turned to see Dad walking in.

"Sir, I'm doing some questioning here," Langley snapped at him.

"I'm the boy's father." Dad was unfazed. "Is he being charged with anything?"

"Oh, pardon me, sir." The detective stood up and introduced himself, shaking Dad's hand, and then briefly explained the trouble with Erik.

"Is my son being charged?" Dad asked again.

"Well, you see, that's what I'm trying to figure out. I just want to ask a few questions."

Dad glanced down at the notepad.

"Looks like you've already done that. Without me here. Or my attorney." Dad reached down, gripped me under my left armpit, and pulled me to my feet. "We'll be going now. My number's in the phone book, home and office. Expect to be hearing from our lawyer, Detective. You too, Langley."

"Be reasonable, we have situation here," Langley sputtered.

"Let's go, Joshua." Dad led me to the door.

When we walked through the office, Li was sitting in one of the chairs, handcuffed. He gave me the slightest of nods, as if to reassure me that he wouldn't say a damn thing to anyone. I felt like a traitor.

When we sat down in the car, I began a faltering and rushed explanation to my dad, and he interrupted me, saying, "Just take it easy for a minute, son. You can tell me all about it when we get home."

"I just want you to know I didn't do anything wrong," I said.

"I know." He started the engine. "You're a good kid."

We drove out of the school lot under a gray sky. The trees lining Main Street swayed in a steady wind. Dad asked if my stomach was upset. He must have noticed I was hunched in my seat. I nodded. On the way home, he stopped at the Gas-Go and got me a Vernor's ginger ale. I hadn't realized how dry my mouth and throat felt until I took the first spicy-sweet drink of it. The bottle was empty by the time we got home, when the first drizzles of rain began to fall.

"Brings May flowers," Dad said absently as we entered the house. "Take off your shoes and come on downstairs. I could use a beer."

I did, but it was strange. The basement was, really, Dad's place to be by himself—at the house we lived in before, he had a "workshop" in the garage that served the same purpose. I'd snooped around there, of course, but never made a habit of it. When I was little, I'd sneak my friends into the workshop to see the model planes and ships Dad built; when I got a bit older, I'd rifle through a box of old *Playboys* tucked into a corner among cans of paint and blacktop sealant. Paul made that discovery first, and later passed the tip on to me. One day, I found the box had mysteriously disappeared. Terrified my transgressions had been noticed, I pretty much stayed away ever since. The invitation to Dad's den felt like I'd been asked to join an elite club, until I headed down the steps. There wasn't the sense of dread, of being swallowed into the belly of something damp and dark that I'd gotten when we'd headed into Mike's basement to see the puma. But something felt like it was shifting, changing, both in and outside of me, as I tromped after him.

The basement was dry and cool. Carpeted and finished with drywall, the room smelled of musty newsprint and the faint astringent tang of airplane glue. A couch sat in front of a cheap plywood entertainment system, its blank TV reflecting us as shadows in the lamplight. Books and records covered a coffee table: Etta James and Cormac McCarthy, Bobbie Womack and James Ellroy. Beer bottles filled a Detroit Pistons wastebasket. Half-assembled models sat on a workbench in the far corner. Dad sat down in a rocking chair beside the microfridge, and gestured for me to take a place on the couch.

"I'm sorry I haven't been paying more attention lately," he said. "I've wanted to give you room to, you know, do your thing. I figured as long as your grades were holding up and you were staying out of trouble, I had nothing to worry about."

Rain pattered on the glass block windows near the ceiling. I didn't understand what he was apologizing for.

"You don't have to worry," I said. "I mean, I'm fine. It's just things have gotten weird lately."

"Since about when?"

"A little before Christmas," I said.

I gave him the run-down on what had happened as best I could, with Apple Boy and Lindsay, Erik and Jason, the parking lot fight, and all that. He sat there listening and nodding, not really reacting much, until I mentioned the biker gang by name.

"The Leatherwolfs? Jesus Christ, Joshua." He took off his glasses and set them on the coffee table. "If your mother finds out, Jesus, we'll never hear the end of it. What have you been doing hanging around them?"

"I haven't been. Do I look like a biker to you?" I pointed at my horn-rims and messy, purple hair. "They're around Jason and hang out at the Farm; I think he got to know them in prison. They freak me out."

"They should," Dad said.

"Wait." I looked him over: a middle-aged, balding insurance man sitting slumped in a rocking chair. "How do you know about them?"

"They've been around forever. Used to be a greaser car club in Detroit before they got into motorcycles, around Western and Clark Park—or was that the Scottsmen? Anyway, it around when the Satan Saints got big. '66-ish. Didn't even know they were still around." He sighed and loosened his tie. "I used to buy grass from them."

I gaped at him as if he'd grown a second head. He cleared his throat.

"That was a long time ago," he said. "Erik's in with them now? God. He doesn't even have a motorcycle." Dad cleaned his glasses with the front of his shirt.

"He holds onto stuff and moves it around for them sometimes." I didn't want to tell him about the time I'd helped Erik deliver, and the whole mess on the boat that day. "Nothing big."

"Using that kid as a mule."

"Kinda. I guess."

"Bunch of assholes. Always were."

My dad almost never cursed around me. Now, down in the basement, talking about how a biker gang that used to sell grass to my dad was using my best friend (who was on the run from the cops) as a mule, I felt like I was in a *Twilight Zone* episode. Any moment the wall might open up to reveal a flying saucer, and Dad would calmly explain how our whole family were refugees from planet Galador, and that's why Paul was so good at math. I remembered the galaxy map in my brother's room. It seemed possible.

"So, what was all that noise about at school today? They found attack plans in Erik's locker?"

"They weren't attack plans. There were for AGB. That game."

"The one you and Erik painted all of those soldiers for a couple of years ago?"

I nodded. Dad helped me detail a squad of northern barbarians when I was in ninth grade. He used a single-bristled brush to add red spatter onto their axes, which I thought was pretty awesome. Later, when Erik got excited about it, I took the credit.

"Did you tell them it was just a game?" he asked.

"It didn't seem to help. Erik made a model of the school for it."

Dad chuckled, and then said, "I'm sorry. I didn't mean to laugh. But that's kind of funny."

"Yeah, well, they didn't think so. They asked if I thought it might be a way to prepare for the real thing."

"There anything to that?"

"Not unless the whole school's floor was painted with hexagons and everyone took turns moving around on them."

"Is that what you told them?"

"No," I said. "Erik can be kind of crazy, and he hates this place, and he hasn't been dealing too well with a lot of stuff. He's been talking about wanting to buy a gun for a while. He and Lindsay took off together for his uncle's cabin by Traverse City today. I told the cop about most of that."

He scratched his chin. "You shouldn't talk to police, Joshua."

"What? Why not?" I flailed my hands in front of me. "I told the truth and did what they asked. Isn't that what you're supposed to do?"

"Maybe. But there are some people you can trust to be truthful with, and to be honest with you, and some you can't. I didn't know that so well when I was your age, either."

"You seem like you turned out alright."

"Sure." He gave a dry laugh. "That's how I ended up in Vietnam."

I felt a burning in my throat and a bad taste in my mouth, thinking of the photo with the dead man. "Like you've been truthful with me and Paul about *that*. You weren't over there filing papers, Dad."

He jerked in his chair and blinked. His face hardened in the silence. I wished I hadn't said it. As he leaned back in the rocking chair, he took a deep breath.

"No," he finally said, his soft tone lifting the weight off my chest. "No, I guess I wasn't."

"Why'd you lie? You could have just told us."

"I didn't want it to affect how you thought of me," he said. "Maybe I shouldn't have kept it from you. It seemed like the right thing at the time. And for a long time, I just didn't want to talk about it. Everybody has things like that." A faint smile crossed his face, and he slowly stood up. "Just a second."

He turned his back on me and plodded over to his workbench. He gently set aside a half-assembled P-51 Mustang fighter and moved a few bottles of model paint, then pulled open one of its drawers. It made a long wooden scraping sound like the pole barn door at the Farm. Leaning forward and peering, he reached his hand inside. Screws, nails, and tools clinked together as he rummaged.

"Dammit," he grumbled. "Ah, there it is. Here, son, heads up."

He spun and tossed a small black box across the room. A little rectangular coffin smacked me in the chest and tumbled into my lap. I popped it open. The medal glinted on silk lining, looking like a Valentine's gift from George Washington, a purple locket of the general in profile.

"A Purple Heart? Wow, Dad."

"Don't be too impressed. It's for getting shot in the ass."

I laughed, and he did too.

He made his way back to the chair and sat down, leaning forward with his elbows on his knees to look at the medal.

"I was running away," he said. "That's why I'm here right now."

He turned in his chair and opened the microfridge on the floor. Glass bottles clinked as he pulled out two Millers. He opened both of them and held one out to me. I set down the box and took it from him, cold and damp in my palm.

I asked, "Do you think Erik and Lindsay are going to be okay?"

He took a sip of his beer before saying, "I suppose. Guess it depends on what you mean by 'okay.'"

"What about—" I faltered and then looked at my beer label, a lady in a red dress swinging on a crescent moon.

"You? You're going to be fine. You've always been a bit ahead of the game. People can be real idiots sometimes. We'll get a lawyer to take any calls tomorrow. It's all going to blow over. A flash in the pan." He patted my shoulder and clinked his beer against mine. "Now let's finish these before your mother gets home."

The beer tasted like piss, like beer always did, but I drank it down to the last drop as we sat in the basement, talking, while the rain came down outside. It was good to be down there with him. Someday I'd get used to the taste of it.

16

School was closed for two days while the cops interrogated everyone they could get their hands on, and reporters descended onto Birch Hills like an occupying army. Erik's model of Birch Hills High ended up making it onto the *Observer*'s front page after all, with his dad's guns placed next to it, adding drama to the photo op. The saga was mentioned on the national news and made all of the papers. The story of a potential conspiracy to slaughter the high school population was pretty exciting for the media, but in the end, there wasn't much to keep it going. Pink Dick was expelled for being disruptive to the educational system, Lindsay too. The rest of our friends were sweat down by cops but let go. Erik wasn't charged with anything, but was committed to a psychiatric ward "for his own well-being." I couldn't help feeling like this was all my fault.

A couple ultra-positive motivational speakers were brought in to do an assembly, and then we all had "Talking 2-gether Field Day," with trust falls and sharing circles and all that crap. It sucked.

Without Erik around, everything felt wrong. We struggled to keep the conversation going at lunch, and I felt obligated to keep tabs on how everyone was doing. I guess I never noticed that's what Erik did in the group. It was hard, because nobody trusted anyone anymore, because nobody knew who had said what to whom, and everybody felt like they had a secret.

I missed Lindsay.

After a day of compulsory games, we were herded into the gym to watch the cheerleaders. The Birch Hills cheer squad were national contenders when it came to sexy athleticism. It was easy to understand why. Their tanned and toned legs kicked and spread. In little, white sneakers, they gave flashes of the banana-yellow hot pants under their skirts as they lifted and tossed one another's lean bodies through the air, weightless and boundlessly enthusiastic. Flawlessly synchronized, every step according to plan, their smiles were relentless, their voices ringing and feminine through the gymnasium—"B! H! H! S! We're the BEST. BIRCH Hills HIGH School. B! E! S! T! The BEST!" They leapt around and hugged one another before falling back into formation. The song "Barbie Girl" exploded from the PA, and the cheer girls danced without a hint of irony, locked into its synthesized beat.

Mike Kahuakai and I sat on the bleachers, gaping. Twitch sat nearby, absorbed in a manga. The top of Mike's head had darkened to a deep umber from a day of forced outdoor activity. He shone with sweat. A serene smile was frozen on his face.

"Are you high?" I asked.

He shook his head.

"How can you smile like that?" I said. "This is insane."

"That's why I'm smiling," he said.

Twitch, the perpetually shaky anime geek, seemed unusually calm.

"What's with you, Twitch?"

Twitch looked over at me and lowered his comic. "Doctor upped my Xanax."

The song ended, and the squad cried out, "*B! E! S! T! Birch Hills High School! B.H.H.S!*"

The mascot, Eddie Eagle, came running out onto the court like a shamanic idol of school spirit, his wings lifted into a triumphant pose, a smile frozen on his beak. There was no way to tell who was inside the costume. This was the thing's first appearance since Erik had broken into the athletic office and taken a dump into its empty head last fall.

People remembered. As Eddie Eagle and the squad led chants of *B! H! H! S!* a vocal minority catcalled another sing-song refrain: *Shiiiit-head! Shiiiit-head!*

Mike, Twitch, and I and joined in, howling along with what

would remain the school mascot's underground nickname for years to come.

With our tenuous connection to the Farm severed, and both Pink Dick and Erik gone, I was always worried we remaining freaks were going to get jumped by jocks anytime, but it never happened. I wanted to think this was because of the new tolerant outlook of our post school massacre era. I doubted it. I think they worried we might shoot at them.

I missed Lindsay and Erik to the point that it hurt, a horrible ache in my chest, and I sat around in my room hating myself and then chastising myself for being so self-pitying. I would not pray.

A week after her expulsion, I got Lindsay's letter.

Dear Josh —

Hey how are you? I hope you are OK. Everything is fucked up really bad here and I don't know what's going to happen. I got expelled from school for skipping but really there just doing it because I was with Erik when he got picked up by the pigs. My mom is keeping me prisoner at home and having my aunt watch me while she's at work. Most of what I know I hear through Amanda, cuz she's the only one who's allowed to see me. Funny since she's more messed up than any of the guys I hang out with. I'm hoping my sister will come from Seattle and get me out of here but I doubt it.

I'm sorry I said you weren't nice. I swear I never did anything with Erik after you + me became something, but I guess that's not really the issue now. When you + me hooked up at that party, I told him I liked you. He said you didn't know that me + him had done it. He asked me if he should tell you or if I should. I said we shouldn't tell you at all. I was worried you wouldn't like me anymore. Maybe that was wrong. I'm not sure.

Erik said that you probably knew I was over at his house that day you brought his book back. Well, I was. I was up and his room and he had his shirt off, that's true.

Erik's whole chest is covered in cuts. You probably didn't know that. He's been cutting X shapes on his body ever since his mom moved out +

he doesn't know why. It's like he does it without thinking about it. He was scared because he couldn't stop + was showing me because he knew I had done stuff like it, but he made me promise not to tell anyone. But it wasn't like what I did. He cut himself where no one could see it. Then you showed up with his book. I promised not to tell anyone, but I was going to make him tell you that day, but they took him away first.

I'm telling you now because he's in a mental hospital so it's not really a secret anymore. I'm sure they found the cuts cuz there were like a hundred of them. You and I both know he never would have gone all gun crazy at school. I'm telling you this not so you'll forgive me but so you'll stay friends with him. He's going to need some good people to be around when he gets out and I think you're a good person. You always try to do the right thing. I wish everyone would be more truthful and less afraid. It would make things so much better but people just aren't usually like that I guess. I wish I'd told you more things. I wish I'd said I love you. Don't bother writing or calling now cuz it might get intercepted. I guess this is goodbye.

Love,
Lindsay

I drove to the truck stop out past the Farm and bought a Maji-Krystal unicorn. I didn't know how else to show Lindsay how I felt. The only other thing I could think of was slitting a couple arteries and then showing up on her doorstep like a lawn sprinkler pumping out Hawaiian Punch. The fact that this would freak out her mom and get me institutionalized would probably earn some points with her, too. As it was, my heart rate still went up when I shaved my neck with a safety razor. Besides, I was the stable one, the good one; I was the Yin to her Yang, or maybe the reverse. I could never remember which side was white and which was black in that thing.

A stern-faced woman opened the door to Lindsay's house. She was skinny as a greyhound, and her hair had been pulled back into a ponytail. She looked down at the boxed glass unicorn I held as if it were a dead rat.

"Hello, ma'am," I said. "Is Lindsay home?"

"I know who you are," she said. "Why in God's name would I let you even talk to her?"

Great.

"I know I messed up," I said. "That's why I—"

"If I'd known what sort of people run rampant in this town, I would have never raised her here. Look at you!" Her face trembled, and her hands formed into bony little fists. "Using her, giving her drugs, encouraging her to commit suicide—"

"Hold on, I never—"

"You never, you never. You nasty little liar. Planning shootings, getting high. You're filth, and I'll make sure she never comes around any of you again."

Waves of rage and pure madness poured off of her.

"Mrs. Kruthers, please—"

"You're filth, and from filth. You reap what you sow."

I set the box at her feet.

"I'm so sorry," I said. "This is for your daughter."

"You'll be sorry yet, young man."

I turned away and stepped off her porch as Mrs. Kruthers screamed after me, threatening me with damnation and jail. I didn't think it could get worse. I was wrong, of course.

The reporters packed up, the crisis counselors went back to whatever useless social work they usually did. Metal detectors were installed at Birch Hills High, along with CCTV cameras, and everyone was issued an ID badge. Dustin Lake was voted Most Likely to Succeed, and Ashleigh Baer was named Prettiest Smile for the forthcoming yearbook. Prom came and went. I didn't go. Erik, Lindsay, and Dick were gone, erased from the picture. The rest of us became invisible.

Weeks passed without hearing from Erik. I was too ashamed and confused to go over and talk to Erik's dad. Especially knowing about his separation from his wife, his past relationship with the hot tub lady, and how his son had landed in the looney bin. I had no idea where Mrs. Grundler had gone.

The next time I saw Mr. Grundler, he was on the evening news, three weeks after they put away his son. It was May 13, a Thursday.

"Just a few weeks after a school shooting scare in the suburb of Birch Hills," said the newscaster, "one of the suspect's parents has been murdered in an apparently unrelated incident."

I looked up from my paperback to see a body with a sheet pulled up over its head being rolled out of a trailer on a gurney. Yellow tape cordoned off the street in Manor Estates trailer park I'd looked down on so many times through my binoculars.

"Fifty-one year old Don Grundler, who gained some fame with the song 'Daisy Chain'…"

On the other end of the couch from me, my dad sat up straight. The newscaster droned on. The trucker had found his wife sleeping with Mr. Grundler. He shot both of them to death with a .38 caliber revolver, then drove out to the lake nearby and turned the gun on himself.

"Oh, that poor boy," my mother said. "Is he still in the hospital? Have you heard from him at all since the meltdown at school?"

Alison, who was on the floor playing with a toy horse, looked up at me and said, "Joshua, why are you crying?"

I ran to my room, threw myself on the bed, and buried my face in the pillows. I heard my mom and dad come into the room. Dad just rested his hand on my back, patting me to let me know he was there, and my mom said soft, comforting things I could not comprehend. Eventually I fell asleep.

I woke up in the middle of the night. Alison had put one of her stuffed bears on the pillow next to my head. I put my arm around it and passed out again.

The next morning, I got a phone call from Erik. I forgot all of the chaos for a moment when I heard his voice. We were talking again, and it made the world seem more normal—even if the reason for the call was anything but.

"Hey," he said, "They're letting me out. How are you doing?"

After a moment, I said, "Fine. You?"

"Dandy. Thanks for asking."

"Wait," I said. "They're letting you out of the psych ward when something really traumatic just happened to you? I mean—"

"The insurance ran out."

"That's horrible."

He laughed. I did, too.

"Hey," he said, "Can I pick you up tomorrow? We can go hang out at Arthur's Pond and then do whatever."

"Erik, Arthur's Pond is gone. Remember?"

The line was quiet.

"It would still be cool to hang out," I said.

"Okay. See you when I see you," and then he hung up.

The month Erik had been in the hospital was the longest we'd gone without seeing one another in years. We'd always had homeroom together. We lived in the same neighborhood, if you could call it a neighborhood. We were best friends. At least, we had been.

We sat on a picnic table at the Heron Lake boat launch, the car's engine ticking as it cooled in the gravel lot. He spun a dandelion between his thumb and forefinger. His nails were painted black and chipped, like Lindsay's used to be. I'd never seen him wear nail polish before. Just after dark, the undulating chatter of tree frogs filled the air, and stars shone on the indigo lake.

Though it had only been a few weeks, it felt like years had passed. I wasn't quite sure where the person next to me was coming from, or why he was there. All I knew was that Erik had been discharged from a psychiatric ward. His dad's funeral was tomorrow. I was pretty sure he hadn't heard about what I'd said about him to the cops, but worried he'd find out.

"So, how was the hospital?" I quickly added, "That was a stupid question. Sorry."

"No, it wasn't. You're fine," he said. "I'm okay. I met some cool people in the nuthouse, actually. And they let me play my guitar and draw. I guess it looks like I'll still graduate, too. Maybe they'll even cut me a break on my grades 'cause of my dad getting killed and everything."

"Maybe. Sharon Tweedy still got an A in Mrs. Stroheiss's class when her mom got cancer. She missed like half the assignments."

"I don't think her mom even died, either."

"She didn't."

"Shit. Sharon Tweedy gets all the breaks. Must be nice."

"Yeah." I pushed up my glasses and fidgeted.

"You know, I knew he was seeing that woman. Her name was Trisha. I caught them together once—it was really messed up— like, a couple days before I turned sixteen."

"Ugh," I said. "Wow."

"Yeah. Anyway, on the day of my birthday, that car was in the in the driveway." He jerked his head toward the lot. "The keys were in the pocket of my leather jacket. Mom and Dad came out and watched me start the engine. They were holding hands, with that huge ridiculous house behind them, taking pictures of me behind the wheel, and my dad just looked so sad, even though he was smiling. And my mom looked so happy to see me smile for the pictures. Because I never do for pictures, you know, but I did that day. For her. And after I took the car, I couldn't bring myself to tell Mom about it." He tucked the dandelion behind his ear. "Part of me thought the car was a payoff from my dad. But part of it was that I just didn't want to hurt Mom. Maybe I was chickenshit. I guess it doesn't matter."

He cleared his throat before saying, "I talked to my mom, you know. About the affairs and the car. Yesterday."

"Oh. I bet that was, um, weird."

"She told me that Dad had planned on getting me a really nice car since I was in eighth grade. They used to argue about it. He just wanted to help me be cool. I mean, he never really said it was an exchange, like hush-money or whatever. I just thought that was how it was supposed to be." He swatted a mosquito against his neck.

"Why'd you think that?"

"Like, I got the car the day after I told him I knew about him and his whore—I shouldn't say that, she's dead now, too—but anyway, I got the car the day after I told him, so what was I supposed to think? But he'd registered it a week *before* that. My mom pointed it out on the papers. They were in the glove box the whole time." He kept his eyes straight ahead when he talked, not looking at me, not really looking at anything. "And you know what? Mom knew he was seeing other people. She said they always had, both of them. They separated because dad was seeing Trisha without telling Mom, and because Trisha was sneaking around, too. Can you believe it? I mean, I thought he was paying me off, that he was lying to my mom, and I hated him for it, and was fucked up about it for years. Now I don't know what to think. And he's dead. It's like, they were the people I'd known longest, my whole life, and I didn't even really ever know them at all. I wonder if that's what it's like for everybody and their parents. Maybe."

"At least you're okay," I said. "They aren't pressing any charges on you for the bulldozer or anything, right?"

"Right." He stood up and stretched, then pulled off his leather jacket and tossed it on the picnic table. "I still don't get how they found me and Lindsay so quickly the day the cops grabbed us, you know? Like, we split right away, and they still got us."

"Not a lot of Acrua NSX's out there," I said, cool as a cucumber. "And they've had it out for you for a long time."

"Yeah," he said. "You're probably right. Do you want to swim?"

"Now?" I laughed, surprised. "I don't have a towel or anything."

"You worry too much," he said.

He pulled off his shirt and undressed. I looked away, but not before I glimpsed the scars all over his chest, stomach, and thighs. The thin X's gleamed in the moonlight. I wondered if he knew what he was trying to cross out. I remembered how I'd yelled at him, "You do it to yourselves," and I cringed.

When I looked back again, Erik was a ghost wading through the darkness, then naked and swimming through the reflected sky.

Our doorbell rang at about nine on the morning of Mr. Grundler's funeral. Alison ran across the house hollering "I'll get it," as if there were any doubt. Every chime of a doorbell or knock on the door was like a Christmas present for her. Her footie-pajama feet padded across the house. The hinges squeaked open, and then she scampered back toward the kitchen, calling me to the door.

I felt the sight of him in my guts: Erik standing there in the doorway, a tie dangling from his right hand. He held out in front of him as if it were a dead snake. It was black, like his suit, cufflinks, sunglasses, and shirt. I was pretty sure he didn't know how to tie it.

"Hey," he said.

"Hey." I still wasn't sure if he knew what I'd said about him at school. I didn't feel scared. I felt horrible. "Nice suit."

"Huh?" He looked down, as if he'd forgotten he was wearing it. "Yeah. I'm all *The Matrix* and shit. So…can I come in?"

"Oh. Sure, dude, come on. We have coffee and eggs and stuff."

The breeze of him passing through the door was so thick with marijuana that I nearly fell over. He wandered down the hall toward the kitchen, still holding the tie out in front of him. Even today, he was leading and I was following.

My mom walked over to him. "Erik," she said, "I'm so sorry, sweetie." She hugged him really tight, and it bothered me for a second. I'm sure she could smell the stuff, too, but she didn't show it. He just stood there until she let go and pulled out a chair for him. "Sit down, hon. I'll get you some coffee. You drink coffee, right?"

He nodded, then sat and absently placed the tie in a pile on the tabletop. I pulled up a chair across from him. Mom breezed out of the room for a second, my guess was to inform Dad that Erik was stoned in our kitchen wearing his funeral suit.

Mom came back and set a cup of coffee in front of Erik, along with the sugar shaker and some hazelnut creamer. "Have you eaten this morning?" she asked.

He shook his head. When he took off his sunglasses, he looked like someone had punched him in each eye. It was from either crying or bong-rips or both. Mom took a loaf of bread from the pantry.

"How's your mother doing?" she asked, dropping a couple slices into the toaster. "Do you have family at the house?"

"We have more family there than we can deal with, but she's okay." Erik sipped his coffee. "For once, the gates on Shady Glenn paid off. First the news trucks came out when I got taken in, and then for this new thing, again."

"Vultures," she said, deep lines forming on either side of her mouth.

"My dad says vultures need to eat, too. I mean, he used to," Erik said. "Their turn'll come around."

The television clicked on in the front room, and the theme from one of Alison's cartoons began to play. Dad's heavy footsteps approached. He came into the kitchen and sat at the table, mumbling a hello to Erik. Erik nodded in return, and then sipped his coffee.

I wondered exactly why my friend was here and not at home with his family. Then I wondered if I could still call him a friend or, more accurately, if I could call myself one.

The Good Guys remained clueless, I'm sure. Erik wasn't a killer, I wasn't a hero, and they were anything but wise. He was just a pissed off kid in a small town, they were a bunch of spooked authoritarians, and I was just trying to do what I was told. They saw an opportunity to show how in control they were of everything. Together, we all got his frightened mother to lock him up for the last month of his father's life. They'd never admit that's what happened. Not even if I wrote it all down and told the world. It made me sick.

The toast popped up, and Mom scraped butter across it.

"Jam?" she asked.

"Yes, please." He set down his coffee. "I'm riding over there myself," Erik said, to no asked question. "I'm going to drive myself there, and nobody can tell me any different."

"I'll go with you," I said. "If you want me to."

Mom set the toast in front of him and gave a look to my dad. He cleared his throat and stood, saying, "Well, then, I suppose you'll need a bit of help with that tie."

Erik gaped at my dad as if he had just used heat vision to immolate a sack of mewing kittens. His expression was a mix of wonder and outrage. After a second, Erik's face fell. He stood up and held the tie out to him.

"Yeah," Erik said. "My dad never showed me how."

About an hour later, I was seated beside him in the black Acura, the air conditioner an endless roar, the smoked windows a tight seal against the bright heat around us.

"Erik," I asked as we turned onto Grand River. "Why aren't you riding to the service with your family?"

"What family?" He snorted. "My dad was an only child, like me. My mom's family all thinks I'm a freak. After years of trying to put me away with the whole 'We want you to go somewhere where you can get the help the you need' bullshit, she finally got her wish, eh?"

"I don't know if—"

"Add to that the fact my dad's dead because his lover's white trash husband murdered him. A fine welcome home from the nut house. I've kind of had enough of my family, thanks."

"I'm sure they never meant to hurt you, I mean—"

"Almost no one *means* to hurt *anyone*. But everybody does. Either because they're selfish, or afraid, or just plain stupid. I'm done with all this shit. Family. Love. Country. Humanity. All of it." He glanced over at me. I couldn't see his eyes through the black lenses, but his voice quavered a bit. "Friends are all I can count on. Right now, I don't have many of those, either."

I didn't say anything. He didn't know what I'd done.

"Thank you for being here," he said.

"Really, it's nothing," I said. "You have nothing to thank me for."

"Pink Dick only has T-shirts, so he's too embarrassed to come. Mike Kahuakai is, though. And Kenzie, fuck if I know why," Erik said. "Li will be there, too. And you, of course. I'm going to sit with you guys."

The car coasted up to a stoplight. A fat man at the Shell station on the corner struggled to open the ice cooler out front. A seagull poked around in the trashcan by the gas pumps. It was a beautiful day.

Quietly, hopefully, I asked, "Shouldn't you should sit with your mom?"

"Have you been listening to me at all, dude?" The light changed and he stomped on the accelerator.

"Jesus, Erik," I said.

"Look. I'm not sitting with my family. Dealing with my cheating dad, my vanishing mom, our bass-akwards school, and this shithole of a town made me insane."

His rant was gaining momentum. I knew there was no point in trying to rein it in right then. He made a hard left onto one of the side streets. The tires squealed.

"My own mother thought I was going to be a mass-murderer. Jesus Christ. Why? Because I wear black and listen to metal. Because I drew some comics and built some models. Fucking Columbine-obsessed assholes. I don't even *like* Marilyn Manson. He wears a boobie-suit. He makes music for mallrats and fat goth girls. Fuck."

He pulled over onto the shoulder and skidded to a stop. Cars zipped by on the road as he yanked up the parking brake. Erik tore off his sunglasses and threw them on the dashboard, then dug a pack of Marlboros from his breast pocket. Slouching in the seat, he cracked the window and lit up. Neither of us spoke for a bit. He sat there and smoked.

"I know I'm not a good kid," he said at last. "But I'm not a monster, am I? I know it's kind of hokey, but doesn't anybody take a second to look a little bit deeper?"

"No," I said. "Not usually."

"I mean, I don't go around spreading STDs and randomly beating up and picking on people, like half the popular 'good kids' do. I tried to talk about this at the hospital and they told me I was antisocial. Well, maybe that's because society sucks. How about that?"

I didn't know what to say, other than, "Your mom needs you today."

"Is that why she moved out of the house without even explaining to me why? Is that why she had me put away? Is that why she thought I was a homicidal maniac? Ask anyone who knows me. I'm not like that. My family...we all failed each other. I'm sitting with you."

"Erik." All of my hair stood on end, and cold chills crawled across me. My throat tightened and I said, "I failed you, too."

"I didn't expect you to write me or anything," he said. "And they wouldn't have let you visit."

"No. No." I would not let myself cry, because I didn't feel like I had the right to. My vocal cords stretched tight when I croaked out, "I told them things about you. I was stupid."

He took a long drag. The cigarette shook in his hand like a leaf on a branch as he exhaled. With his red-rimmed eyes staring dead ahead, he asked, "What are you talking about?"

I told him.

I suppose I could have let him sit with me through the service. He would have thought of me as his One True Friend. Mrs. Grundler wouldn't have ever ratted me out. Perhaps years later, they'd reconcile, and he'd still think of me as the one who stuck it out with him through thick and thin. But that wouldn't have been the truth. And the thought of seeing Mrs. Grundler in the front row of the funeral, mourning her dead husband without a son by her side because I didn't say anything—I knew I couldn't live with that. I was going to be torn apart no matter what. So was he. I figured it might as well be because of the truth.

When I finished telling him about what I'd said that morning in the front office, he replied with one word. He didn't sound exasperated, or angry, or despairing. Blank-faced and staring out the windshield at nothing in particular, he only sounded confused.

He asked me, "Why?"

"I don't know." The answer hung there, empty as the black hole I felt howling in my chest.

Truly, I didn't know. The easy answer was that I thought he'd been with Lindsay that day I went over to his house, and I was angry about it. But I knew he'd been with her before, and the fact that he'd been with her again didn't seem like something that should have upset me as much as it did. Maybe I was just tired of feeling like his sidekick. Or maybe after all of the shootings in the news, Erik's anger and misanthropy didn't seem so harmless anymore, and the Good Guys convinced me I should be afraid of my own friend. Now, I could only shake my head, my eyes hot and stinging with tears, and breathe.

An ice cream truck lumbered past on the road outside, chiming out the first two bars of "The Entertainer" in a continuous loop. Erik turned and stared at me.

"You don't know. Well," he said, "could you maybe take a fucking guess?"

"I told you. I was stupid. Like you said."

"I never said you were stupid."

"You said people hurt one another because they're stupid, or selfish, or afraid." I swallowed a hard lump in my throat. "I was stupid. Maybe the other things, too."

"Wow," he said. "Have you been taking notes?"

"I always listen to whatever you say."

"Why?"

I shrugged.

"Oh, yeah, I forgot. *You don't know.*" He put his sunglasses on. "Shit, man, what if I'd had been holding a package for the Farm? I'd be in prison."

"You promised me you wouldn't be doing that anymore."

He grimaced, then said, "You don't know why you told them all that about me. What am I supposed to do with that?"

"What do you want to do?"

"I want to bust your fucking head in. But I already got a funeral to go to." He released the parking brake. "Maybe we'll talk about it later."

We never did.

Erik sat with his mom at the funeral. I sat with Kenzie, Li, and Mike. Lindsay wasn't there. It was more crowded than I'd expected.

The casket was closed and surrounded with flowers. Standing among them was an acoustic guitar with a chipped red heart painted on the pick guard, a gold record, and tons of photos. Don Grundler with James Brown, and Donovan, and what I thought was Peter Tork, but wasn't sure. Don Grundler shirtless with a dark, bright-eyed toddler on his shoulders: Erik. Don and his wife's wedding photo, she in a strapless gown, he in wide lapels, neither of them wearing shoes, and a score of other moments throughout his life. As people filtered in and left trinkets at the casket, pausing to offer condolences to Erik and his mom, Mr. Grundler's exuberant voice sang out through the parlor's speakers.

A new sun is a-risin,' children are realizin'
It's better to be mellow all the same.
Baby, the lesson is you ain't no possession,
Don't go buyin' into that silly game.
Come on, come on, come on, join the daisy chain...

A few of the people in the seats swayed back to the music, and a few clapped their hands to the beat.

"Isn't this from that rap song? P-Crew or something?" Kenzie whispered to me.

"That was a sample," I said. "This is the actual song."

Erik gave the eulogy. He retold a few of his favorite memories of his dad and recounted his father's better traits, none of which I'd ever heard him talk about before. If he cried, he didn't show it. I'm sure the sunglasses, and the fact that he was high out of his gourd, helped with that. The speech was rambling and ad-libbed until he pulled a crumpled notecard from his back pocket. Erik looked at it for almost a full minute before he began reading.

He said, "My father made choices and had friends. And some might say the friends and choices he made cost him dearly, and they led him into a place he should not have been. These choices were his own, however. Who are we to judge, or try to comprehend, what goes on in another man's heart? We must persevere and choose to believe in his goodness, because it is the best option we have. Belief in God is irrelevant if we don't first believe in humanity." He paused, looking down at the card as if he'd lost his place. Erik's voice was nearly a whisper when he said, "I loved my dad, and my dad believed in love. Thank you all for coming."

He sat back down next to his mom. She held him as his shoulders shook, weeping. The funeral director came up and said there would be a reception at the Masonic Lodge, and people would have a chance to share any memories of the departed there. There would be no burial service.

Erik came over and said hello to his friends once he pulled

himself together. He struggled out of his tie, and said he wouldn't be going to the reception.

"That was a good eulogy," I said.

"Yeah," Kenzie said. "It was really, I don't know. Smart, I guess." Li nodded and said, "Yeah."

"Well, nice to know I have some skills. I'm a hit at funerals." He smiled. None of us laughed.

"Do you guys want to go burn one?" Mike finally stammered out. I laughed at that, and so did Erik.

"Yeah, fuck it," he said. "Why not."

Li and Kenzie took off while Mike, Erik, and I sneaked out a side door.

We climbed up on the monkey bars in the park across the street behind the funeral home. Some little kids were playing hopscotch, and Erik said he didn't know kids played hopscotch anymore. Mike said he wanted go play hopscotch with them, but the kids were probably afraid of strangers, and any adult who saw would think he was some kind of perv. Then he lit up a joint.

Three hearses were parked behind the building across the street, waxed and detailed, black and brilliant. The summer sun's reflection exploded across their hoods like a supernova frozen in deep space, and I thought of the galaxy poster in Paul's room with its YOU ARE HERE arrow pointed at a single infinitesimal speck, and I remembered Captain Fiji the Apple Boy sinking into the pond and how Erik had said, "I wonder who's next?"

Erik sat with his suit coat slung over his shoulder and his legs dangling over the edge of the bars. He pointed at the three hearses across the street. "Check it out. That's one hearse for each of us."

"I call the one with the little flags on the front end," Mike said. "'Cause I'm proud to be an American." He took another long drag off the joint.

"I think you have to be a war veteran to get a ride in that one."

"No problem," Mike rasped out before exhaling. "I bet there'll be another war before too long."

We all laughed.

Erik asked me, "Did you ever show your dad that picture we

found in the library book? The one with the dead man?" I shook
my head. He said, "Good."

Mike said, "A picture is worth a thousand words," and passed
the joint to Erik.

"That's what I hear," I said.

"If that's true, why does anyone bother writing anything down?"
Erik pushed up his sunglasses.

"I don't know," I said.

"I wish we could go to Arthur's Pond right now. It's so weird.
It's just gone."

He passed the joint over to me, and I lifted it to my lips. The
smoke smelled of summer and childhood. I held it in for as long as
I could. After a moment, I asked, "Do you know where Lindsay is?"

"Gone," he said. "Gone and lost forever. She's not allowed to see
me anymore. Not allowed to see any of us. We're the Bad Guys."

Mike sang the chorus of "Too Late for Love" by Def Leppard
and hung upside down on the monkey bars. His shirt fell down
toward his face and showed a big jiggley belly. His uncle loved Def
Leppard, he said.

I watched the sun on the hearses and loved sitting there in
playground with my friends and not having to talk. Across the
park, kids hopped around and laughed. Then I remembered how
Erik knew I sold him out and wondered if he'd forgotten, and then
I realized he probably didn't care right now, and I wanted to hug
him and I wished Lindsay were there, too. And I was so stoned.
I had to pick up my graduation cap and gown tomorrow. Then I
remembered that a new millennium was around the corner, so I
asked Mike, "Do you think the world is going to end?"

"God, I hope so," he said, smiling and pie-eyed.

"Haven't you been paying attention?" Erik lit a smoke. "It
already has."

epilogue

When I saw Erik's car for sale at a used lot on Grand River, I knew he was gone for good. Erik's black NSX, which had rammed the gates of Shady Glen, smuggled contraband for the Leatherwolfs, and served as the steed of Birch Hills High School's own Antichrist, was advertised as "Super Clean" in neon pink letters across its windshield. We'd gone everywhere in that car. Now it waited to be bought without memory or history, only mileage.

My parents had given me a car of my own, a "surprise graduation present," in July. It was a used Ford Festiva, previously owned by my vegan lesbian cousin. It had two irremovable bumper-stickers: one read, "Animals are People Too," the other, "Dairy is Rape." The first one I sort of understood, but the second one bewildered me. I never fully understood it. I'd seen cows milked on my Uncle Peter's farm. So had my cousin, for that matter. At no point did our uncle ever rape a cow as part of the milking process. Maybe if it had said, "Dairy is Third Degree Sexual Misconduct" I could've seen it. But that would've made the sticker gigantic. It couldn't have been worse than being trying to meet girls that summer with the word "rape" in big red letters across my Festiva's bumper. I painted over it, eventually, but the stuff was always flaking off.

That last summer before college was a lonely one for me. Lindsay was gone; I found out from Amanda she'd been sent to live with her aunt in Tennessee. I never got another message or a call from her.

Mike Kahuakai's house got raided by the cops a week after school let out. Someone must have tipped off his dad first, because they found a totally empty basement. I don't know what happened to all the growing equipment and the weed. I think the puma manifested a couple weeks later when two prize-winning Bay horses were found half-eaten in their stables a few miles from our subdivision—one of which was owned by Ashleigh Baer, the other by her sister, Brittany. Everyone agreed it had been a cougar attack until someone called up Channel 7, claiming to be a werewolf and taking responsibility.

The news actually ran with the story; a graphic of a howling wolf in silhouette with the word "Werewolf?" sat beside the newscaster's head as he explained the grim possibility. They even interviewed someone from the Wayne County Department of Mental Health, who discussed the recent upsurge in LSD usage, and how this could lead to lycanthropic fantasies and violence. Then, they cut to a Birch Hills family therapist, who suggested it might have something to do with "Satanists using the Internet as a recruiting tool." A man from the Department of Natural Resources, with poorly concealed contempt, countered, "There are several large predators, native or invasive, more likely to kill livestock than werewolves." And then he added, to clarify, "Because werewolves aren't real."

Mike and his dad moved out in the middle of the night a few days after the raid. I never met, or even saw, Mr. Kahuakai. One day I knocked on his door to see if Mike wanted to go to a movie and found the house was empty. Even the overflow of junk mail was gone from the mailbox. It was as though he'd never been there at all.

Kenzie moved to Royal Oak and managed one of the family's jewelry stores there. His parents threatened to write him out of their will if he didn't get a job. Li went to live with his cousin in Chicago, where he spun records in clubs as "DJ Chigger." It felt as if aliens were snatching up everyone I knew. An imperfect rapture had carried away only the most fucked-up to the promised land of "Somewhere Else," leaving me behind.

I didn't see Erik very much that summer, either. He ended up a part of the Farm crew again, joining a metal band with some other stoners who practiced in their dilapidated barn. He and Pink Dick, who never finished his senior year, both played guitar. There was a changing of the guard going on out there, and I was sad to see Erik becoming something of a leader among them.

The run-in on the boat had kept Erik away for a time, but Jason had been arrested for braining a liquor store clerk over the head with his cane when his debit card didn't work at the register. He took his whiskey and walked out without paying. In the eyes of the law, he'd committed armed robbery. Jason De Groot, a paroled felon, ended up on the fast track back to prison. René used this opportunity to borrow Jason's car for a road trip from which he never returned. The enigmatic Travis, along with some of his biker friends, packed up and headed somewhere out west. The Farm was free of its primary operators, whatever that had entailed.

Erik and his band became the Farm's main characters. They named themselves The Schoolyard Gunmen, and were actually quite good, if you liked that sort of music. The smattering of burnouts and bikers who still lived out there were happy to have the band hang around; they brought girls out to the property and provided entertainment for their parties. It wasn't a place I'd ever liked to be, but Erik had made it his home.

He'd managed to graduate, but Erik's time in Birch Hills had broken him—not that he'd ever been all that together in the first place. It wasn't the drugs or alcohol that really bothered me. He was a teenager, with a recently murdered parent, who played guitar in a band called The Schoolyard Gunmen—I mean, what could you expect? But the light had gone out of his eyes, his voice was ragged, and his hands perpetually shook. He emanated damage.

Erik brought up his dad's murder in some way or another every time I saw him. I couldn't really blame him for that, either. People talk about their troubles, whether they mean to or not. He knew I didn't like the Farm, so we really just got together to catch up a handful of times that summer. We'd get blown out, drive places, and then just sit down and talk. I'd quit getting stoned but made an exception for him. We were hanging on to something that was already over, and we knew it, but we still had fun. Most of those voyages are lost in the haze. They run together, like damp watercolors placed in a stack. We always ended up at the boat launch on Heron Lake, just a few feet away from where his dad's killer had offed himself. I don't know why.

"Me and the band are going to hit the road in the fall," he said. "Wish us luck."

"Cool," I said. "Remember me when you're famous."

"Hell," he laughed out, "I think I already had my fifteen minutes."

I got a letter from Erik a couple months after I started college. My parents forwarded it to my dorm. The yellow envelope contained a snapshot of him sitting barefoot and cross-legged on an oriental carpet. Dressed in an elaborate kimono, he held the stem of a hookah pipe between his pursed lips. A pair of gold-framed Elvis sunglasses glinted beneath the dirty shag of his hair. A chubby blonde with a pretty face and a nose ring sat beside him, resting her head on his shoulder. Her huge boobs stretched a black Schoolyard Gunmen T-shirt to its limits, and her eyes fixed on the lens with a red stare. Erik and the girl smiled their oblivion through the photograph's celluloid window.

A postcard of Amsterdam Central Station accompanied it. Written on the back, in his frenzied jagged hand, was: *Bet you wish you were here! — Erik.*

Maybe he was being sarcastic. It was nice to see the Schoolyard Gunmen had attained an international audience of at least one person, though.

I kept that photo tacked up on my dorm room wall. Other than yearbooks, it was the only picture of Erik I had. I didn't have any address for him, his mom sold their house and moved away, his cell phone number didn't work, and he never answered my emails. After we graduated high school, he just vanished.

I ran into Lindsay Kruthers at Bigmart a few years later. I was back in Birch Hills for the summer after my fourth, going on fifth, year of college. I'd switched majors from English to journalism to creative writing. I co-hosted a punk rock college radio show with my sometime girlfriend, a feminist poet with cat-eye glasses and a drinking problem. Recently, I'd become the first undergrad to work as a co-editor of the school's lit journal. My GPA was a 3.8, which was hard to maintain while also holding positions on the Student Government Board, College Democrats, Students for a Green Earth, and the College Gamers Guild. People knew me as a dependable guy who was happy to help out. I bought organic produce. I responsibly drank microbrewery beers, jogged daily, and had recently adopted a meditative practice to counteract my anxiety attacks. My parents' insurance covered my ulcer medication. My hairline was receding. I was twenty-three.

When Lindsay called my name down the kitchenware aisle, I was trying to decide if I should buy a George Foreman Grill. I didn't recognize her at first. Her hair was dark and cut short. I never assumed Nuclear Red was her God-given color, sure, but it was strange to see her as a brunette. She wore a pair of khaki shorts and a white blouse. Her thin diamond tennis-bracelet matched her earrings, as well as the sparkling rock on her left hand. The scars on her wrists had faded. What threw me most, though, was the baby stroller.

"Lindsay?" I asked, not because I wasn't sure, but because I struggled to accept it.

"Ohmigod, how are you?" She leaned forward to hug me, but the stroller was in the way. She was behind it, and I was to her right side, so we both leaned over the thing and gave each other one of those one-armed bullshit hugs, complete with rapid back-patting. I stared down at the baby. It looked like a tiny Winston Churchill in a blue sleeper, holding its right foot in both hands. The baby looked up at me, cooing stupidly as bubbles of spit burbled from its mouth. After four or five back pats, the embrace mercifully ended, and we dumbly faced one another.

Lindsay still had that amazed look on her face. I was in town for summer break and went to Bigmart. She was the one with the tennis bracelet and the wedding ring and the baby stroller. What she had to be shocked about, I had no idea.

"Hi," I said.

"I haven't seen you in ages! What are you doing here?"

"I was thinking of getting one of these grills," I replied.

"Oh. You should. They work really well." She looked around the aisle as if lost. "What've you been up to?"

"I'm home from college for summer break. You?"

"Oh, God, so much has happened," she said. "Where to start? I got married, for one."

"Congratulations."

"His name is Charles. He's in real estate." She giggled. "He's wonderful. And this is Evan." She smiled at her baby.

"Wow," I said.

"Yeah," she said. "I almost didn't recognize you. You look so different. So, I don't know, normal."

It hadn't occurred to me that I looked different than she remembered. My mom had thrown away my old tweed coat before I went off to college. My hair was a sandy brown. I'd gotten tired of dying it random colors; I'd practically been through all of them, and it just felt kind of silly—especially now that it was thinning. In jeans and a white button-down, shopping for kitchenware, I must have appeared shockingly normal. Just like she looked to me.

We said a few more random things, agreed we should catch up some time, didn't exchange numbers, and then we hugged again. I'd totally forgotten the reason I'd come to the store. We walked down to the opposite ends of the aisle and turned the corner.

I burst out of the store's air-conditioned glare and into a hot July twilight. The automatic doors wooshed closed behind me. I crossed the black lake of the parking lot and then hopped into my little Ford Festiva, which still resentfully clung to life. It was getting late, but I didn't want to go back to my parents' yet, so I just drove around for a while. The radio played the same "classic" rock songs it had for years, and probably always would. I passed the Taco Bell where Erik got beaten up and the Gas-Go where I got mine. Almost nothing had changed.

I had stayed on the right track. I did what needed to be done and was doing just fine. There were problems, sure. Some nights I couldn't fall asleep, or a fire in my stomach would wake me just before dawn. Sometimes I felt suffocated by my own life, or like my life wasn't even my own—the sorts of things you learn to keep to yourself, I guess.

I drove past the park downtown. A group of bored-looking kids sat on the concrete planter, slouching in too big or too small clothes and dragging on cigarettes, just like we all had done a few years ago. I slowed down, as unobtrusively as I could, to look at them. There was a skater or two, a thin, bleak-looking kid in black, a fresh-faced girl in torn fishnets, a rapper guy, some dude with pink hair that fell into his eyes, a few others. I didn't recognize any of them, but it seemed like new actors had been recast into the same roles.

The kid with pink hair stood up and playfully pushed one of the others. Now that he wasn't sitting hunched over on the planter, I could see his T-shirt: the words *Schoolyard Gunmen* above a stenciled AK-47. The other guy had painted on the back of his hoodie, in between the lines of a giant X, BHHC. *Birch Hills Hard Core.*

I hooted with laughter, but not for long.

ABOUT THE AUTHOR

Geoff Hyatt has shown intermittent enthusiasm for electric guitars, vintage psychedelic posters, and ginger ale. He moved to Chicago after surviving the millennium, where he often sits reading a book while waiting for the bus.